Praise for Hilary McKay's Casson family

'It does what we hope JK Rowling would do: it makes everything you wish for come true, including the unlikeliest of outcomes.' *Sunday Times*

'Witty, warm and humorous . . . family reading par excellence.' *Carousel*

'Warm and witty.' *Financial Times*

'We are so fond of this fresh, funny, foolish, wise, real family.' *The Horn Book Magazine*

'Just the sort of crazy family you ache to be a part of.' *The Good Book Guide*

'Funny and touching.' *Guardian*

'A crazily fantastic story with loads of mad and hilarious moments.' *Independent on Sunday*

'Warm, witty and wise, with unfeasibly broad appeal and proven anti-depressive properties, I would give this book to 9-year-olds, teenagers and their parents.' *Sunday Telegraph*

CADDY'S WORLD

Hilary McKay

h

Hodder
Children's
Books

A division of Hachette Children's Books

For Sophia and Victoria Steinsberg,
with lots of love from Hilary McKay

Chapter 1
Charmed Circle

These were the four girls who were best friends:

Alison . . . hates everyone.
Ruby is clever.
Beth. Perfect.
Caddy, the bravest of the brave.
('Mostly because of spiders,' said Caddy.)

Alison, Ruby, Beth and Caddy had started school together aged four and five, plonked down at the four corners of a blue-topped table in Primary 1.

'You four will be friends,' the teacher had told them, pronouncing the words like a charm. She was an elderly person, tall, with silver-streaked hair twirled and looped about her head, black beads, and, remembered Caddy, years afterwards, a sort of purple haze about her that may or may not have been a cardigan.

She was probably a witch.

'You four will be friends,' she said again, and her glance included all of them: Alison, who was sulking, Ruby with her thumb perilously close to her mouth, and her hair cut short like a boy's, and Beth, who was not only perfect, but also dressed utterly and completely in brand new clothes, snow white underneath, school uniform on top. Last of all Caddy, who had arrived very late because her mother had forgotten the date.

The teacher smiled down from her looped and beaded heights at the table of little girls. Charmed, they smiled back up into the ancient purple haze. Alison, Ruby, Beth and Caddy: bewitched.

Alison lived next door to Caddy, in an immaculate house. No visiting went on between the families. Alison's mother used to look out of the window at Caddy's mother, and shake her head and say, 'I'm not getting involved.'

'Absolutely not,' Alison's father would agree.

They were both estate agents. Sometimes Alison's father would gaze at the state of the Cassons' roof and murmur, 'I hope we never have that property on our books. You'd have to be honest.'

Their daughter was honest naturally. Alison's was a lovely but insulting honesty that conceded to no one.

Her bedroom window faced Caddy's but usually she kept the curtains closed. 'I like my private life,' she told Caddy. All the same she was a helpful friend. When Caddy showed signs of oversleeping on school days she had several times flung slippers and hard-nosed teddy bears at her window and screeched, 'Get up!'

'You could work out a much better system than that,' said Ruby. 'You'd only need two pulleys if you could fix a pendulum to the lamppost in between. It's out of line, but it wouldn't matter if you hung weights or something to take up the slack . . .'

Ruby, although she still sucked her thumb, was brainier than ever. Ruby, small, red-headed and quiet, owned a hammer and a Swiss Army knife, loved books and maps and numbers and patterns and words from other languages. She was good at mending things too. Ruby knew how to fix charms on bracelets, chains on bicycles, and frozen computer screens with petrified mice. She was an only child, both her parents were dead, killed in an accident when she was a very small baby. Then an amazing and unusual thing had happened. Her four grandparents (all retired, all elderly, all astonishingly intelligent) had pooled their not-very-large savings and bought a house. And into it they had moved with Ruby. All four of them. So Ruby was brought up with not much money but with lots of books, nursery rhymes in five different languages, kitchen chemistry, seaside expeditions to observe the effect of the moon on the tides, and a large floppy cat, bought in order to stop her feeling too much of an only child. Really though, it was her friends who did that. They shared with her and teased her, and at school they stopped her ever having to do a thing by herself. That was very useful to Ruby, because as well as being brainier than ever, she was also shyer than ever.

Perfectly happy though, until the day of her last school report.

Just like all her friends, Ruby had ripped open the brown envelope and unfolded her report the moment she left the school gates.

The first time she read it (eyes round with disbelief), she thought, *how amazing!*

The second time, with Caddy reading over her shoulder, she thought, *but awful!*

She became aware that her heart was beating very fast.

'Ruby!' Caddy had exclaimed, when she finally understood the report's staggering conclusion. 'Do you think you'll do it?'

Ruby did not answer at once. The pounding in her heart was now so loud it seemed strange that Caddy did not hear it too. Her astonished mind was still tottering between AMAZING and AWFUL.

'It would change things a lot if you did,' said Caddy, and then noticed the frightened look on Ruby's face.

'Don't worry!' she exclaimed. 'We'd still be friends! Just as much . . . in a way.'

Ruby's stared at her, eyes wide and shocked.

'You'd be posh!' said Caddy, and laughed a little, to encourage Ruby to laugh too.

'Posh!' repeated Ruby.

'I was only joking. Anyway, you already are, a bit. Well, you've got a posh cat! So, will you do it? Would you like it?'

By now, Ruby's heart was bumping less fiercely. Her mind had stopped its tottering between AMAZING and AWFUL. It came down firmly on the side of AWFUL.

'No I wouldn't like it!' she said. 'And I won't do it!'

'Don't you even . . .'

'And I don't want to talk about it, either! So there!'

'I don't see why . . .'

'Please, Caddy,' begged Ruby.

'All right,' said Caddy.

Beth. Is perfect.

'I'm not,' protested Beth, neat-haired, brown-skinned, modest as well as perfect. 'I'm not . . . If I told you some of the things I think . . .' Her voice trailed away. She never would tell. She was ungrudgingly nice, even to her little sister Juliet (who preferred the name Jools and was far from perfect).

Beth's parents were also perfect. Her mother was good at homework and cakes for school fairs, and her father always won the fathers' race on sports day. To complete this perfection, and best of all, there was a pony named Treacle, a perfect birthday surprise that had appeared when Beth was eight.

'Of course, he's to share,' Beth was told at the time. 'When Juliet's old enough.'

Juliet was nine now, and Beth would have shared, but, 'No thanks very much!' said Juliet.

Last of the friends came Caddy. Cadmium Gold Casson. Caddy had no special label. She wasn't perfect or clever and she didn't hate anyone. For a long time she was just Caddy, which bothered her friends.

'Just Caddy is fine,' protested Caddy. 'It's what I am.'

All the same, they found her a label, mostly because of her fearlessness with spiders. Caddy was sorry for spiders, so universally unloved, and she did not allow them to be squashed.

'Leave them to me,' she would command, and no matter how grey-legged, scrabbling, or hairy, she would gently pick the monsters up and carry them to a place of safety.

'Caddy, the bravest of the brave,' said Alison, Ruby and Beth.

'I'm just Caddy really,' said Caddy, but she liked having a label all the same. She felt it gave her a proper place in the circle of friends.

'Alison, Ruby, Beth and me,' she would say to her little sister and brother, Saffron and Indigo, and told them stories about Treacle the pony, Wizard, Ruby's enormous cat, and the tank of miniature fish they could sometimes glimpse through Alison's bedroom window: tiny rose and blue flickering things, like swift-trailing flames.

'I call them The Undead,' said Alison.

'*Oh, Alison!*'

'Well, they do die.'

'Then what do you do?'

'Scoop 'em out, and put some more in,' said Alison. 'Don't look like that! It's life.'

Alison was a fatalist. She could live with the possibility of almost anything. For years she had lived in a house with a For Sale board outside and neither protested nor questioned its existence.

Her friends had been appalled when it appeared.

'But where would you move to?' they asked. 'Not away?'

Eight-year-old Alison had shrugged.

'Find out!' they ordered.

'How?'

'Ask, of course!'

Alison, after a good deal of prodding, had asked. She had even gone so far as to half listen to the answer.

'Near where my uncle lives,' she reported.

'What uncle?'

'The one who came to visit.'

'Well, where does he live?'

'South, somewhere.'

'Lots of places are South!' said Caddy. 'Half of everywhere is South!'

'It began with T, or something.'

Ruby found a map and located Tamworth and Toddington.

'Which?' she wondered.

'It might not be either,' said Alison.

For a year or two that was that. Nothing happened. The For Sale board stayed where it was. And then, one day a new name floated into view.

Not Tamworth, or Toddington.

'Tasmania,' said Alison.

'*Tasmania?*' asked Ruby. 'Are you sure?'

'Yeah,' said Alison, yawning a bit, but even she was shaken when Ruby appeared the next day carrying a small plastic globe.

'This is here,' said Ruby, pointing to a tiny reddish-coloured island, chewed-looking at the edges, and surprisingly close to the North Pole.

'Is it?'

'Yes, and,' Ruby turned the globe upside down and pointed again, 'that's Tasmania.'

Alison blinked a bit at that. And then she took the globe into her hands, found the chewed red island for herself, turned it over, peered. Sure enough, there was Tasmania.

'OK,' she said.

'But don't you mind?' shouted Caddy. 'It's the other side of the planet!'

'Tasmania, Tamworth,' said Alison. 'Who cares?'

'But what about us? We'll still be here. How can we be friends?'

'Why shouldn't we be?' asked Alison, honestly puzzled. 'What's Tasmania got to do with it?'

Another year passed, and a new joke began:

'When Alison goes to Tasmania . . .'

It meant an incredibly far-off time, impossible to date. Probably after the discovery of life on Mars, but before the death of the Sun. Once Ruby did some research and found hanging lakes, pink grass, and a mythical beast called a Tasmanian Tiger.

'You're mixing it up with Mars,' said Alison.

By the time another year had passed, they had forgotten the joke. Alison's For Sale board had become part of the landscape. The charmed circle held, as strong as it had always been.

'We are friends for ever,' Caddy told Indigo and Saffron, and believed it was true.

Caddy needed a for ever. There was no for ever at home. There it was as if from time to time a genie from a bedtime story picked their world up in his hand and spun it on his finger. People set off on journeys and returned unrecognisable, vanished for days, came to live in your bedroom, hid under tables for hours and hours, wandered the house fast asleep demanding to go home, counted pennies in jam jars till they had enough to buy bread, and the next day gilded halos for the school Nativity play in real gold leaf. Caddy's home was a turmoil of sound, colours, piled possessions and lost belongings.

'You could always clear up a bit if you don't like it,' remarked Alison.

'It's exciting. I love it,' said Beth.

Ruby, who sometimes found it a bit of a burden being the only one under seventy in a house of five people, said, 'You should try being an only child like me.'

'I was,' said Caddy. 'For ages and ages.'

Caddy could still remember very clearly the world before Indigo and Saffron had arrived. In those days her father had been home nearly all the time. Whole weeks would pass in which no tears were shed, no heads were clutched, no vases were stuffed with apologising roses, no hard sums were done to prove the cheapness of renting a place to work in London compared to the enormous cost of building a soundproof, childproof studio at home.

In those days nobody ever wore dark glasses and explained they had hay fever.

And then Indigo and Saffron arrived a year apart, and if Indigo was a surprise, Saffron was an unlooked-for and cataclysmic shock. And it seemed to Caddy that no sooner had they found her a place to sleep (Caddy's room) than the head clutching and hard sums that had begun with Indigo's appearance suddenly stopped. (Although the roses and the dark glasses did not.) The matter was decided. Her father would work in London, renting a studio, coming home on Friday nights.

All at once there was one parent at home, instead of two, and three children, instead of one.

Time passed.

Caddy got used to Indigo and Saffron, and then very fond of them. Her father stayed away more and more often, for longer and longer periods. Caddy got used to that too, and to the tears when he left, and the way her mother scrambled through the days and nights, juggling people and painting and children and cooking and always a bit behind with everything.

'Darling Mummy is not the world's best at multitasking,' said her father, on one of his heroic trips home to unscramble the household.

'Darling Bill,' Eve would say, and collapse on the sofa to read fairytales to the children while Bill restocked the fridge and the freezer, wrote lists, threw out junk, constructed star charts for good behaviour, stared at the bills and gave everyone lots of very sensible advice.

'Darling kids,' Bill said once, pausing from filling bin bags to gaze at them, good as gold, curled up on sofa cushions, listening to stories. 'Aren't we a nice little family?'

'Little?' asked Caddy. It was June and warm but her skin prickled, cold with alarm. She did not know her father thought they were a little family.

'Little?' she asked again. 'I thought you thought we were a very big family. Too big to fit in even a single hamster! That's what you said.'

'Cadmium darling,' said Bill teasingly. 'You're not going to start taking life seriously, are you?'

The genie in the bedtime story frightened Caddy sometimes. She pictured his smile as he lifted their world to play. Tonight the genie's smile was on Bill's face: sweet, and teasing and ruthless, as if he was the one who spun their world on his finger.

'When are you going back to London?' asked Caddy rudely.

That wiped away her father's smile, but it didn't touch the genie's.

'One day,' said Caddy's mother, soon afterwards. 'Not now, not soon, not for ages, wouldn't it be lovely and exciting . . . ?'

It was another hint of change, and this time Caddy ignored it. She had had enough of change. If she could have chosen a world to live in, it would have been the world inside her glass snowstorm. The snowstorm held a small, square house with a blue front door and a yellow garden path. No bunches of roses were ever delivered. No one ever slammed the door, or paced the garden path, backwards and forwards. Nothing changed ever, except the weather.

'Perfect,' said Caddy.

'You're the only person I know who would like to

live in a snowstorm,' said Alison. 'The only one!'

'Only-Ones' was a game the girls played now and then.

Alison herself had a good only-one. She was the only one to have actually seen a ghost. Quite clearly too, in the graveyard next to her grandmother's house, a young man in old-fashioned clothes peering through the gloom of a November afternoon to read the inscription on a gravestone. Alison had watched as the young man bent to pick a wintery daisy, looked up, caught her eye, hesitated and vanished. This event had happened more than a year before, yet so far no one had been inclined to stand where the ghost had stood and read the inscription on the gravestone.

'It would seem too nosy,' said Beth. (She was the only one who would have thought of such politeness to a ghost.) She was also the only one to have met royalty, at Sandringham one Christmas. 'Thank you. Aren't you cold?' the Queen had asked, accepting her ribbon-tied Christmas roses.

Ruby was the only one to have been in an ambulance, lights flashing and sirens wailing, Ruby herself utterly thrilled despite a broken arm and a bumped head, not only with the ambulance ride but also with the fact that she had proved conclusively that it was possible to jump higher than the safety net on Juliet's trampoline.

'Did you see?' she asked everyone afterwards.

'Yes, yes!' they reassured her, in case she felt the need to do it again.

Caddy herself had many only-ones. The only one to have been in a house while a baby was being born: Indigo, a Sunday morning surprise. Caddy, aged six, had been given a pink toy camera for surviving this ordeal, and had spent many frustrating hours afterwards trying to make it work. A year later (when she had become the only one to have acquired a sister, aged three, with zero warning), her father had remembered her disappointment and somehow from amongst the turmoil produced and handed over a real camera, the one-use disposable sort, but better than pink plastic.

The camera, coming as it did just after Saffy's arrival, had been exactly what Caddy needed. Home was in chaos, but here was the key to a bright new future.

Caddy had packed a small bag, stolen a dog she found tied to some railings, and become the only one of the four to run away from home. She had not been found until the smoke from her campfire was seen rising above the laurel bushes in the park. She had then become the only one to be taken home in a police car, protesting all the way that she was not lost, she didn't need returning, she was a wildlife photographer and had the pictures to prove it. Nobody took any notice, although later, when the film in her camera was developed, she was shown to have been telling the truth. Caddy still had those pictures: several ducks, a squirrel, a blackbird's nest and a water vole.

'Wow!' said Ruby and Beth (and even Alison) but they were glad she was back and hugged her a lot.

'Don't run away again,' they said, and for years and years, Caddy didn't.

Chapter 2
Lost Property

The summer that Caddy was twelve, the summer that followed the days when Eve had said, "Wouldn't it be lovely and exciting . . . ?' and Bill, with his genie's smile, had asked, 'Aren't we a nice little family?', that summer, there came a summer storm that rocked the trees and flooded the drains in the streets.

When the deluge stopped at last the girls gathered at their outdoor meeting place, a low wall in front of a house at the crossroads on the way to school. A great consultation began, with Beth saying, 'Who will come swimming with me this afternoon? I've got to look after Juliet and that's what she wants to do. I can't bear to take her on my own. Not after last time! Do you think that lifeguard would recognise me if I wore a different swimming costume?'

'No, of course he wouldn't,' said Ruby. 'He probably hardly looked at you. Too busy clearing the pool! I can't come though. I'm going to the library.'

'Haven't you enough books in your house already?'

Ruby laughed, assuming it was a joke to suppose that any single house could hold enough books to outlast such a deluge as they had just survived.

'Do Beth a favour!' suggested Alison, inspecting her newly varnished deep purple fingertips. 'Take Juliet with you. Do you like my nails?'

'Lovely,' said everyone.

'Three coats. It took ages. Caddy, I'm sure you had those jeans on before it started raining!'

'I did. I've been wearing them all summer. I'll come swimming with you, Beth! I'm not scared of that lifeguard! And he needn't have gone on like he did about Juliet. She couldn't help choking and it was only Coke!'

'Three cans, little pig!' said Alison.

'Anyway, it wasn't Beth's fault! Let's all go swimming, and then nail varnish shopping and to the library on the way home.'

They were in the middle of trying to persuade Ruby and Alison to agree to this plan when something caught their attention. A movement in the rain-washed litter at the base of the wall.

'Oh, yuk!' said Alison. 'Oh revolting! Oh no, Caddy!'

For Caddy (bravest of the brave) had already picked it up. A featherless new-hatched bird, washed from its nest in the yew trees high overhead.

'It's twitching,' said Beth. 'It's still alive.'

'You can see its veins,' remarked Ruby, but she too flinched away from its frog-fleshed coldness.

'I don't know how you can hold it,' said Alison to Caddy, almost crossly, because the thing was so awful, and yet so helpless.

It twitched again, jerking its pulpy, purple mound of a body, its naked wings flailing, and it stretched out a reptilian neck and opened its beak in a long soundless shriek. On a nearby lamppost two pink and grey doves looked resolutely in the opposite direction, disowning responsibility.

'You would hardly guess it was supposed to be a bird,' said Beth. 'I don't think you should have picked it up, Caddy. I'm sure you're not meant to do that. If you leave them alone their parents come and take care of them.'

'That's fledglings,' said Caddy. 'When they have feathers and can hop about and keep themselves warm.'

'What are you going to do with it then?'

'It ought to go back in its nest. It must be up there somewhere.'

They stood back to gaze into the dim green

depths of the yew trees.

'You couldn't even prop up a ladder,' said Ruby. 'Not in all those skinny branches.'

'Can't we take it to a vet's?' asked Beth.

'I did that once before,' said Caddy. 'And they took it into a room and came out about one second later and said, "Very sorry, it just died," and they wouldn't tell me what of, or if they'd tried any medicine, or anything. I always thought afterwards they murdered it. What we need (I know you'll all moan) is one of those long stretchy ladders like they have in the fire brigade . . .'

The howls of her friends drowned the rest of her sentence.

'You can't call the fire brigade *again*!' said Ruby. 'They'd be furious! Think how they were about that frog in the drain last Easter! You got that awful letter!'

'They were nice the first time though, when we found the squirrel we thought was an escaped monkey . . .'

'*You* thought was an escaped monkey!' corrected Ruby.

'You can't do it again, Caddy,' agreed Beth.

'What are we going to do with it then?' asked Caddy, and Alison peered at the wheezing, gaping blob in Caddy's hands and said, 'It'd be better dead.'

Ruby and Beth nodded in agreement.

'Yes, but it's not,' said Caddy helplessly. 'So we'll have to look after it somehow . . .'

'We?' asked Alison, while Ruby shook her head and stepped backwards in alarm.

'It's you who's good at looking after things, Caddy,' said Beth.

'I'm not!' protested Caddy. 'Any of you could do it just as well . . .'

'My mother would go mad if I took it within a mile of the house,' said Alison.

'I've got a cat,' Ruby reminded Caddy.

'I don't think I could,' said Beth. 'I haven't time. Not with Treacle to look after. It looks cold, Caddy.'

'It *is* cold,' said Caddy, 'and I've nothing to wrap it in. I'd better take it home . . . if it *is* me, taking it home?'

Her friends looked guiltily away.

'All right,' said Caddy.

'Do you really not mind?' Ruby asked her a little worriedly.

Caddy was never entirely sure what she believed animals and birds could understand of human communication. More than people guessed, she suspected. Perhaps even this poor fledgling could grasp something of the debate that had gone on around it.

For this reason she said bravely, 'Of course I don't mind! I love it! I just didn't want to grab. I'll take it home then. Thank you! Any of you can visit it, any time you like!'

Even Alison blushed a little at that.

After Caddy left, the afternoon seemed empty. Her friends drifted off in different directions, feeling a little lost. All courage to face the swimming pool deserted Beth without her.

'I'm not taking you there,' she told Juliet. 'And you needn't sulk! Anyone who sicks up three cans of Coke in the deep end of the swimming pool and has to have the whole place cleared shouldn't *want* to go!'

Alison wandered round the shopping streets until boredom gnawed her like a pain. She found herself calculating the days left until term began. It seemed a terrible thing to her, to be looking forward to school. She went home and painted her nails again, this time a dark and savage red.

Ruby also thought of school, remembering her last school report. The memory made her change her mind about going to the library.

'I can't ever go there again,' she said, and to save

herself from temptation, dropped her library card in a bin. It vanished immediately among the cans and takeaway wrappers. For a little while afterwards Ruby could not see very well.

It was not the first baby bird that Caddy had rescued, although easily the most forlorn. Her mother groaned when she saw it. Too well she knew what the next few days would hold. There would be name choosing, food making, sleepless nights, panic, bargains with God, rage, tears, a funeral and struggles with the difficulty of gravestone construction.

'The swallows lived,' said Caddy, who could never forget the pair of fledgling swallows from the fallen nest she had found two years before. She had fed them on flies and grubs and they had gobbled and stretched, fluttered, preened and flown from her hands to join the spiral of birds circling the street. It had been the proudest day of her life. It was the reason why she tried so hard with each new patient, and cried so hard with each new failure.

The baby pigeon was installed in a shoe box on Caddy's bedside table. The box was lined with cotton wool for softness, and dried grass for an authentic smell of the wild. Saffron and Indigo looked on with interest, and offered to help.

Caddy left them in charge while she went in search of baby pigeon food. Indigo worried about the mother pigeon left behind.

'Do you think it's very sad?' he asked.

Saffron thought about that. 'No,' she said at last. 'She probably saw Caddy taking it away and thought, Oh well, I shan't have to bother, and was quite pleased and went off and did something good.'

'What sort of good?'

'Like went to the park.'

'Oh,' said Indigo, comforted.

Saffy peered critically at the occupant of the shoe box. 'I hope it gets its feathers soon,' she remarked. 'It makes me feel funny looking at it. I don't like being able to see its insides from its outside. Or that yellow baggy bit.'

'It smells too,' said Indigo, lowering his voice in case the bird should happen to hear and understand.

It did. Sweetish and slightly rancid.

'Like lost property,' said Saffron.

'What?'

'It smells like lost property at school. That big box full of old clothes and lunch boxes and shoes and things. I hate it when I have to look in there. I wouldn't like to smell like that.'

'Poor Lost Property!' said Indigo. 'Let's call it

24

Lost Property, Saffy! And let's give it a bath before Caddy comes, to surprise her.'

Caddy arrived back only just in time. The bathroom hand basin was full of warm water. Strawberry-scented bubbles had been fluffed up by Indigo into a strawberry-scented cloud. Lost Property was just about to be lowered to his fate when Caddy grabbed him from Saffron's hands.

'You stupid kids!' she exclaimed. 'What do you think you're doing? You might have killed him! Murderers!'

'Indy and me are not murderers!' said Saffron indignantly.

'We wasn't hurting him, Caddy,' said Indigo earnestly. 'We've been looking after him all this time!'

'Looking after!' repeated Caddy scornfully, as she tucked Lost Property tenderly back into his box. 'Poor little thing! He might have drowned!'

'He wouldn't! Of course he wouldn't, would he, Saffy?'

'Do you think we didn't know he had to breathe?' Saffron asked Caddy witheringly. 'Do you think we wouldn't have held his beak up?'

'Hmm,' said Caddy, crouching over the shoe box.

'What are you doing with that paintbrush?'

'Feeding him.'

'What?'

'Oatmeal and water and scrambled egg. I was scrambling the egg. That's why I took so long.'

Already Caddy's flash of anger had passed. She had a temper like a firework, a bright fizz of flame, a few bangs, a little smoke and a shower of sparks, and it was over. Now she was using a tiny pointed paintbrush to drip oaty eggy mush in the baby bird's beak. She looked up proudly at Saffron and Indigo when a drip actually went down.

'He's swallowing! Did you see?'

They nodded, impressed.

'We'll have to think of a name for him.'

'We already have. Lost Property.'

'Lost Property?' repeated Caddy.

'Indigo thought of it.'

'Well,' agreed Caddy. 'I suppose it's true. He is.'

For a day and a night Lost Property occupied all their time. They hung over him, willing him to live. Indigo shaded his shoe box with branches to make him feel at home. Saffron told him comforting stories about pigeon picnics in the park. Caddy detected an infinitesimal growth of feathers. They were all sure that he knew his name.

And then he died.

Eve promised Heaven as the logical conclusion.

Saffron and Indigo, old hands at the job, surveyed the garden for an unused burial plot and dug a large hole.

Caddy wailed, "I tried and I tried.'

'It was just too young,' said Eve, sniffing herself as she hugged her. 'I didn't think it could live from the first.'

'Why didn't you tell me then?'

'What would you have done if I had?'

'I wouldn't have bothered,' said Caddy. 'I wouldn't have made it a nest. I wouldn't have fed it. I wouldn't have let it have a name. I wouldn't have loved it.'

She cried and cried. She cried so much she spoiled the funeral. Saffy and Indigo, who had expected a good deal of praise for the excellence of their digging, were completely ignored.

'That hole had *corners*,' said Indigo, 'and she didn't even notice!'

'She can dig her own hole next time,' said Saffron.

Chapter 3
The Spinning World

Caddy went to bed exhausted by emotion and funeral arrangements, and was woken at dawn by Alison pelting tennis balls at her bedroom window.

'Hurry up!' ordered Alison when Caddy emerged from under the covers to complain. 'I knew you'd forget!'

'Forget what?'

'Ruby's birthday thing. It's today!'

Ruby's actual birthday had been in the last days of the school term. Presents and birthday cake were over long ago. However, her birthday thing was still to come. It had been arranged by her four grandparents: a trip to the seaside, travelling by train. All four girls, and all four grandparents. They would go exploring, and find somewhere interesting to have lunch. It was a treat, although it didn't feel like it to either Alison or Caddy at not-much-after-six in the morning.

'Today! Oh no! Oh, say you've made a mistake, Alison!'

'Meeting at the station at half-past seven,' said Alison grimly.

'*Half-past seven!*'

'Other people have discos,' said Alison bitterly. 'Cinema trips. Sleepovers. I've tried and tried but I can't think of a good excuse not to go. Neither can Beth. I suppose you could say you've got to stay and look after that pigeon creature.'

'It's dead,' Caddy told her sadly.

'You're stuck too then,' said Alison, and slammed shut her window.

It was a strange day, full of alien activities. Fossil hunting, rock-pooling ('Just explain again what I'm looking for in this hole,' demanded Alison), ordering Italian food in an Italian restaurant in proper Italian with no pointing at the menu, and a visit to the fairground where they were encouraged to work hard at the rifle range, accurate shooting, according to Ruby's grandparents, being wholly a matter of the use of correct breathing techniques.

Now and then, photographs were taken, very fast, with minimal posing. A single click, and there they were, squinting into the sun, arms looped around each other's shoulders, hair tangled and blown in the salt-flavoured wind. Behind them, as one grandparent aptly remarked, the thousand sparkling smiles of the sunlit ocean.

That was the grandparents' favourite picture of the day. They took it home, cropped it, enhanced the blue of the sky, edited out some Italian tomato sauce drips from Ruby's front, added a relevant and lovely quotation from Homer and printed off a copy for each of the girls.

'Perfect!' they said, displaying them to Ruby.

Ruby inspected them doubtfully, chopped off the quotation and took them with her when she went to meet her friends the next day.

They were gathered together in the storage part of Treacle the pony's hay- and straw-filled stable.

'Oh,' they said, when Ruby handed out the photographs, and 'Thank you,' and 'What was it you cut off?' but they did not say 'Perfect'.

'Caddy looks awful,' observed Alison.

'That's because I had hardly any time to get dressed!'

'You could have put *something* on . . .'

'I did!'

'. . . Anything, except those jeans! Anyway, I didn't mean that sort of awful. I meant miserable. Like you are about to burst into tears.'

'I don't!' said Caddy indignantly. 'I was a bit sad, that's all. I kept remembering Lost Property. All those seagulls and him dead before he had a single chance to fly.'

'Pigeons don't fly,' said Alison. 'Not if they can help it. They wobble round the streets eating chips and chewing gum. Anyway, it's not just you who looks awful. I look terrible too!'

That was true. Alison, who loathed above all things having her photograph taken, had only joined the group at the last moment, after a good deal of lurking in the background looking stroppy. Never before had Alison spent a day in the company of four old-age pensioners. The photograph caught her in the middle of muttering, 'I'll die if we meet anyone we know from school.'

All the while that Caddy and Alison had been talking, Beth had been scrutinising her copy of the picture. It filled her with dismay, and it confirmed a fear that had been growing in her mind all summer. She asked, 'Do I really look like that?'

'What d'you mean?' demanded her friends.

'Enormous!'

'No!' exclaimed Caddy and Ruby at once.

'You're not enormous,' agreed Alison (and Beth looked up in relief, because in matters such as this Alison could always be trusted to tell the unsoftened truth).

'You're just quite tall and so much riding has given you a bit of a big b—'

Caddy got to her feet, tipped Alison on to the floor and piled hay bales on her stomach.

'You're lovely and tall,' said Ruby comfortingly to Beth. 'I wish I was. I don't even come up to your ears. None of us do.'

Beth hid her face in hay and groaned. Alison sneezed and writhed until Caddy pulled her up again. Ruby climbed high above the rest of them on a wobbly pillar of bales and inspected her own copy of the photograph. She was in the centre of the group, one arm around Caddy's shoulder, the other clutching Beth's. She looked like she felt she might be swept away if she did not hold on tight.

I do, thought Ruby, gazing at the picture. I do feel that.

The morning passed. One by one the photographs disappeared. Only Caddy's made it home (where it was squirrelled away at once by Saffron as an illustration to her favourite sort of stories). The rest were posted between hay bales, hopefully to be chewed up by mice. Ruby remained on her pillar of bales, silent and thoughtful. Caddy and Beth brushed Treacle, one each side. Alison picked hay out of her hair and said,

'I'm bored. I hate this. And the whole summer's gone. Do you realise it's school next week?'

Ruby flinched.

'This is all we ever do,' continued Alison. 'Last summer, and the summer before, and the summer before that, we were here just like this. Same old hay! Same old spiders! Beth, don't you ever get fed up of brushing that horse?'

'No!' said Beth, clutching Treacle.

'Well, I get fed up of watching you! Caddy, aren't you bored? Wouldn't you like a change? Something different? Amazing or scary or awful? Anything but this!'

For a moment the cold breath of the genie touched the back of Caddy's neck.

'No I wouldn't!' she told Alison. 'I would like things to stay just as they are for ever and ever and ever.'

'Boring,' said Alison. 'Boring, boring, boring!' and left.

Caddy, Beth and Ruby looked at each other uneasily after she had gone.

'Why did she have to mention school?' asked Ruby, while Beth buried her face in Treacle's silky neck and said, 'I will never get tired of you! Never, never!'

Caddy rubbed the shivery patch on the back of her neck, jumped to her feet, and broke the spell. 'Nothing need change!' she said. 'She's only being Alison-hates-everyone. She can't help it. Come on, let's catch up with her. We'll take Juliet swimming and make Alison come with us.'

'She never will,' said Ruby, nevertheless beginning to clamber down from her tower.

'She will. She's bored. She'll do anything! Hurry up, Beth!'

Beth gave Treacle one last hug, and two minutes later they were tearing after Alison, encircling her, jumping round her, saying, 'Come on! Come on! Just to please you, we're taking Jools swimming! Scary and awful! That's what you wanted! Go on, admit you're scared now!'

'Shut up! Go away! I hate you!' said Alison, completely back to normal again.

In the last few days of the holiday, summer grew old. Dry leaves fell and collected in corners in the streets and gardens. The swifts that had swooped and screamed around the rooftops since April vanished in one windy night.

Beth and Juliet were hauled round the town in search of school uniform.

Alison had a tantrum in a shoe shop.

Caddy's mother said, 'Goodness, school!' and gazed

at Caddy, Saffron and Indigo, and asked, 'What about your hair?'

'We're growing it,' they told her.

'Lovely,' said Eve. 'Well. Can you still see out all right, Indigo darling?'

'Mmmm,' said Indigo. 'Anyway, Saffy chops bits off when I can't.'

'Does she?' asked Eve, rather taken aback. She wondered if she should try and stop this cheerful, co-operative, and economical behaviour. How would one do that? Order, 'Never again!'? Lock away all scissors? Would the order be enforceable, or the lock-away practical?

'When I'm doin' it,' said Saffy, reading her mind. 'I use those scissors with round ends that don't cut very well. And Indigo covers up his eyes with his hands. Next time you can watch if you like.'

'I should love to,' said Eve, hugging them both.

'Beth's sister Juliet cut Beth's hair the other day,' remarked Caddy. 'In the night, really though. Not the day. While Beth was asleep. For revenge, Juliet said.'

'Revenge for what?'

'For Beth making her feel guilty. Being so kind, and taking her swimming when she'd been sick in the pool the time before. It made Jools feel awful, all that niceness, she said. It made her mad too.'

'What did it look like?' asked Indigo, round-eyed at this story. 'Beth's hair, after Juliet cut it. Did it look good?'

'It did on one side.'

The kitchen filled with giggles. Saffy, who knew Juliet from school, told the story of her attempt to launch herself from the coat pegs and fly. Indigo remarked that he really could fly, down the staircase, in dreams, and was surprised and pleased to hear that Caddy and Saffron and Eve could do the same. It was decided to telephone Bill, to see if he also had the ability. They did, and he could.

'The whole family!' gloated Indigo, amazed and delighted.

'Let's not ask anyone else,' urged Saffron, not wanting it to be a universal talent, and everyone understood, and agreed.

'When Aunty Linda and I were little girls...' began Eve.

'Did you fly down the stairs?'

'It was nearly as good as flying down stairs! What we did was to pile a whole lot of cushions and things at the bottom of the stairs, and get our sledges...'

'We don't have sledges!'

'Any big old tray would do, that metal one with the roses on would be perfect!'

A noisy, bumpy, laughter-filled evening followed. Caddy went to bed happy, and finding Saffron still awake began a story.

'AlisonRubyanBethanme . . .'

The world felt safe. Caddy completely forgot the memory of the genie's chilly breath on the back of her neck that morning.

There was nothing to suggest or hint or warn that once again he was about to pick the world up and spin it on his finger.

Chapter 4
Absolutely Nothing to Worry About

The genie struck without warning the night before the new school term.

It began when Eve insisted on early bed.

'For everyone,' said Eve. 'You too, Caddy!'

Caddy looked at her in disbelief. The last hour of the evening was her most precious part of the day. Then Indigo and Saffron (aged six and not-quite-eight) were packed away upstairs, and for a little while she had her mother to herself.

'Peace at last!' Eve would say, and they would flop down on the sofa together with great sighs of relief. It was their time for doing nothing at all except enjoying the end of the day; fire-lit in winter, green-smelling in summer, now in September tingling and expectant with the spiralling winds of autumn. It meant a great deal to Caddy to have that little time of peace at last.

'You don't really mean early bed for me too, do you?' she asked.

'Just this once.'

'With Indigo and Saffron?'

'Yes,' Eve seemed preoccupied. 'All of you together tonight.'

'But *why*?'

'I have so many things to do.'

'What things? I'll help you! Don't I always help you?'

'Don't argue, Caddy darling,' pleaded Eve.

Caddy did not argue. Instead she became silent and stiff with indignation. Eve began hurrying Saffron and Indigo upstairs. Indigo looked back sympathetically at Caddy as she dragged slowly after them, but Saffron was bouncy with pleasure. Caddy and she shared a room, and she hated the dismal wait alone before Caddy came up to join her. Often it lasted so long that she gave up completely and left her bed to crawl in with Indigo instead. Indigo never minded that. Saffron was warm, her hair smelled nice, and she banished the dark with murmured stories that began 'One-sapon-atime' and never, so far as Indigo knew, reached an end. He was always fast asleep long before the bears came home, or the prince found his way to the rose-hidden castle, or the dwarfs returned from the diamond mine.

The stories that Saffron told were always fairytales. The ones she liked best, however, the ones she could not tell by herself, were the Caddy stories that began, not 'One-sapon-atime', but 'AlisonRubyan Bethanme . . .'

Usually, all Saffron had to do was recite the opening line and Caddy would begin, but this night it did not seem to work.

'AlisonRubyanBethanme . . .' began Saffron hopefully, the moment they were both in their beds.

Caddy growled, and scrunched over to the wall, as far from Saffron as possible.

'You read a story then, Mummy,' ordered Saffron. 'Read to all of us. Indy can come in with his quilt.'

'Not tonight,' said Eve. 'I have to telephone Daddy. Please be good, Saffron. Give me a kiss and say night night!'

'Oh well,' said Saffy resignedly. 'Night, night. I love you. When're you going to die?'

'When I'm a hundred and ten,' replied Eve, not flinching at this question because Saffy asked her every bedtime.

'How old will I be?'

'Eighty-two and a half . . . No more talking now. Goodnight, Caddy darling!'

'It's not good,' said Caddy.

'I must go,' said Eve hurriedly, and turned off the light and left them. They heard her cross the landing to whisper to Indigo, and then the closing of a door, then nothing at all, only the traffic outside.

'Caddy?' said Saffron.

'Shut up!'

'AlisonRubyanBethanme?'

'NO!' snarled Caddy, gathered herself in an uncommunicative ball, screwed shut her eyes and became an absence in the room.

Saffron sighed, rolled out of bed, and headed for Indigo. Caddy heard him murmuring, 'I been asleep for hours,' and Saffron, undaunted, 'One-sapon . . .'

'Not the beanstalk,' protested Indigo sleepily.

'. . . a-time . . .'

'Not the bears again, either.'

'No. Listen! One-sapon-a-time in a land far away . . .'

'Mmmm,' agreed Indigo.

'There was a king and a queen. And there was a lot of fairy godmothers and one of them was a bad one. And she had black and green bony wings in the picture in my book so they didn't invite her to the party . . .'

'Was there a party?'

'Yes, because I forgot to say one day the king and queen had a beautiful little . . .'

Caddy pulled her pillow over her head and started to cry.

That was how the night began.

Much later Caddy woke, or half woke, to the sound of footsteps. Heavy crunching footsteps on the gravel path outside. Racing footsteps on the stairs. She struggled to understand through sleep that lay as heavy as a blanket on her face.

There were voices, urgent but subdued, and then:

'Absolutely nothing to worry about!' Caddy heard suddenly and quite distinctly.

It sounded like Bill, her father: his voice.

'Daddy?' wondered Caddy, and knew she was wrong, and it couldn't be. Bill was in London, being an artist. He had a studio there, shared galleries there, schemed there, worked there, juggled his money there, had a whole life there that Caddy knew nothing about. At home he lived another life, quite different, another sort of juggling (and not nearly so much fun).

'*Absolutely nothing,*' repeated the voice, '*to worry about, at all!*'

It sounded exactly like Bill, and what was more, Caddy, struggling to emerge from the blanket of sleep, had a very strong feeling that the words had been spoken to her, in her room. Still, when she finally managed to open her eyes there was no one there. What there was, transfixing, inexplicable, was blue light, pulsating on the bedroom ceiling.

And also sounds were everywhere, suppressed whispers, doors opening and closing, an engine, a sigh.

It was over so quickly that Caddy, who had never been properly awake, gave up the struggle and allowed sleep to engulf her once again.

Ages later, it was morning.

'Absolutely nothing to worry about!' said the voice again, and it was daylight, and there was Bill Casson with his head round the bedroom door.

'Daddy!'

'I arrived in the night,' said Bill. 'I—'

From the kitchen came the clatter of tumbling china, and shouts of warning from Indigo. Bill's head vanished as quickly as if a string round his neck had been jerked.

'Don't touch anything!' Caddy heard him call, and then his footsteps running down the stairs, a thump, a howl as he hit the loose patch of carpet on the third step (as familiar as their own skins to those who lived in the house), a crack (that was his head against the hall wall), the kitchen door, raised voices.

'What's happened?' shrieked Caddy, suddenly

frightened. 'What is it? Why are you here? Where's Mum?'

Indigo answered that, his clear little-boy voice floating up from the kitchen. 'Mummy went away in the night.'

The clatter that had sent Bill running was a whole shelf of china, yellow with white spots, brought down in an avalanche caused by Saffy climbing the kitchen dresser in order to find her mug. Now she was poised barefoot among the fragments, marooned in a sea of broken china.

'Good grief! Good Lord! Good Heavens!' complained Bill, on his knees with the dustpan and brush.

'Mummy went away?' repeated Caddy, now at the kitchen door, her voice high and panicking. 'In the night? Why did she? Where did she go?'

'She—'

'What's happened? Is she ill? Have you had an awful row and she's run away? Tell me!'

'No!' exclaimed Bill. 'For goodness' sake, Caddy! Didn't I already tell you? There's nothing to worry about. Really! I promise! Saffy! Stand still, can't you, until I've got the floor clear. What on earth you had to climb up there for, I don't know!'

'I was getting my strawberry mug,' said Saffron, holding it up so that Bill could see the strawberries, and then drinking air from it, to prove it was a mug. 'I always have my strawberry mug in the mornings, don't I, Caddy?'

'I don't know and I don't care,' shouted Caddy. 'Tell me where Mum is *now*!'

Bill, still on his hands and knees, spoke as if he was choosing words very carefully.

'She's just had to . . . to disappear for a little while . . .'

'*Disappear?*'

'She didn't feel too good after you'd gone to bed last night. So she telephoned me and I came back from London and then Mummy went off to good old hospital . . .'

'*HOSPITAL!*'

'. . . where she is now, feeling much better already . . . Saffron, please, don't try to help. You'll cut yourself. We don't need any more bloodshed . . .'

'*BLOODSHED!*'

'CADDY! It's a figure of speech! Stand *still*, Saffy! And explain to me if you can why of all the blasted mugs this family owns you had to go climbing after that one.'

'For my coffee.'

'You don't drink coffee! You're not allowed coffee! Does Mummy let you have coffee?'

'No.'

'Well then!'

'You're not Mummy.'

'TELL ME!' bawled Caddy, hating them both. 'WHAT HAS HAPPENED!'

Indigo, who had been standing quietly watching all this time, said suddenly, "It's the baby.'

'*What* baby?'

'The firework baby, of course.'

'*The firework baby?*'

'Caddy, Indigo, hush!' commanded Bill. 'First we will clear up this mess. Then I will make hot chocolate for all of you. And after that we will talk very calmly about what happened with nobody getting upset because there is nothing to be upset about . . .'

But Caddy's eyes were on Indigo, the only person in the house who seemed to know any answers.

'The firework baby got born in the night,' said Indigo.

That was the latest whim of the genie for the Casson family. The reason for Bill's aren't-we-a-nice-little-family and for Eve's dark hints. That was the coming catastrophe, which Caddy, after one outraged protestation, had successfully managed to forget all summer.

'No, no, no!' wailed Caddy. 'I don't believe it.'

'Caddy darling, you've known since June,' said Bill.

That was true. Eve had broken the news of the new baby to all three of them together. 'I think it is very lovely and exciting,' she had said bravely.

Indigo and Saffron had stared at her, astonished into silence. Caddy, absolutely horrified, had protested, 'Not another baby!' as if there had been dozens.

'Not *another*?' Caddy had begged again (repeating, although she did not know it, her father's exact first words on hearing the news).

'Yes,' said Eve. 'Another baby. We are so, so lucky.'

'When? When? When?' demanded Saffron and Caddy asked flatly, 'Does Daddy know?'

'Of course he does,' said Eve, noticing how Caddy backed away from her hug. 'And not for a long time, Saffy. Not till November.'

'When is November?' Indigo asked.

'When we have fireworks,' Eve told him.

She could not have said a better thing.

'Fireworks!' exclaimed Saffron, and pranced at the thought.

'I *love* fireworks!' declared Indigo, passionately. 'Will there be fireworks when the baby is born?'

'Dozens!' said Eve.

'Rockets?'

'Yes,' said Eve firmly.

'And sparklers we can hold?'

'Yes,' said Eve. 'For this baby, yes! Rockets and sparklers!'

'Is it nearly time for November?' pleaded Saffron and Indigo. 'Is it? Is it?'

Eve had looked at Caddy, now backed against the wall. 'November is wintertime, and this is only just summer. So not for ages and ages and ages and ages,' she said consolingly.

Caddy had been consoled. In June, November was hard to believe in, another world away. She made up her mind not to think about it, and she managed this, mostly very successfully, all summer. Her father did the same, as often as he could. Even Indigo and Saffron, after a few days of waking up and hoping for instant winter, put away the dream of fireworks and the baby with the one of snow and Father Christmas.

But now this.

'It's much too soon!' protested Caddy, there in the kitchen with the broken spotty china, and everyone watching her to see what she would say, 'It isn't winter! It isn't November yet! It's too bad. It's not *fair*!'

Indigo, spooning up dry cereal, with his milk in a separate bowl because that was the only way he liked it, almost understood.

'It isn't firework night,' he agreed.

'We could still have fireworks,' suggested Saffron hopefully. 'Couldn't we have fireworks?'

'Of course,' said Bill.

'Today?' demanded Saffron. 'Now?'

'When Mummy comes home,' promised Bill.

'Tonight, then?'

'Well,' said Bill, 'well, Saffy darling, you have to understand, Mummy will be staying in the hospital with the new baby . . . So probably no fireworks this actual night . . .'

'I want Mummy,' said Saffron in an ominous and explosive voice.

The last fragment of china that Bill picked up stabbed him so that he winced. Nevertheless, he kept his patience.

'Of course you want Mummy,' he agreed. 'You want Mummy and me, and Caddy and Indigo, and the new baby . . . Let's make plans! What shall I do with you today?'

'Aren't we going to school?' asked Indigo.

'School!' cried Bill, like a man falling into sunlight. 'It's school today! Good Lord in Heaven, I forgot!

School! Wonderful! Let's make that the priority! What do you need for school?'

'Coffee,' said Saffron, holding out her mug.

Bill made coffee for Saffron without complaint. He discovered school bags and sweatshirts and clean socks and pencils. He polished their shoes, brushed their hair, forgot their teeth and stuffed their pockets with dinner money. He answered, with cheerful calm, a hundred firework-related questions. He swept up crumbs, watched the clock, found the car keys and gave a great sigh.

'I told you there was nothing to worry about!' he said triumphantly to Caddy as he bundled her out of the door.

Chapter 5
Treacle and Beth

Beth was also getting ready for school, in company with nine-year-old Juliet. Unlike her sister, nobody had ever suggested Juliet was perfect. She was bit of a show-off, a bit of a grabber, and more than a bit dim when it came to understanding other people's feelings. She came down to breakfast on the first day of term in Beth's beloved cowboy boots, the fringed, embroidered ones that had been her last birthday present.

'Who said you could wear those?' demanded Beth.

'Can't I?'

'Of course not. You'd ruin them. They stain really easily. Take them off!'

'You've grown out of them,' said Juliet, not taking them off, and she plonked herself down at the kitchen table and began constructing a very large Swiss cheese sandwich.

'*Juliet!*'

'You said ages ago how much they hurt your feet.'

'I didn't. I don't remember that at all. They're much too big for you, anyway. And actually, I was wanting to wear them today.'

'Oh yes?' asked Juliet sceptically, her voice slightly muffled by bread and cheese. 'I bet you've only just thought of that. And I know they're too small for you because there's bloody marks inside where they rubbed your heels!'

'That was because I had the wrong socks on! That was the only reason. Give them back!'

'Oh, all right,' agreed Juliet, kicked them off in two loose, easy kicks, stood up, stretched, and curved slowly backwards until she achieved a crab position (still chewing) with her hair puddled in a heap on the kitchen floor.

'Sugar Puffs,' she remarked, upside down, unlooped, and came back to the table.

Beth ignored her and pulled on the cowboy boots. She was pleased to find they were rather less painful than she remembered. She paced exploringly about the kitchen.

'Absolutely perfect,' she said.

'I was only recycling them,' remarked Juliet, now pouring Sugar Puffs into a bowl. 'You have to recycle things to save the planet. Which yoghurt do you want, strawberry or cherry?'

'I don't care.'

'I'll have cherry then,' said Juliet, and ate her Sugar Puffs with one thin brown hand curved around the cherry yoghurt tub, in case Beth should change her mind. By the time their mother came down from the shower, hurrying to be off to work, she was scraping the bottom.

'Packed lunches,' said their mother, pulling boxes of sandwiches and apples from the fridge. 'Don't forget to clean your teeth! Have you both had proper breakfasts?'

'Mmm,' replied Beth, cautiously sampling her second spoonful of yoghurt, and keeping her boots out of sight under the table.

Juliet said, 'I haven't had a banana yet.'

'Hurry up, then!'

'Or any toast.'

'Beth, do you think you could be an angel and pop in some toast for Jools? And you will remember to lock up?'

Beth nodded. Their mother always had to leave before the girls. It was Beth's job to lock the house each morning, and take care of the key all day. She had done this for years, since before she was smaller than Juliet. Beth was responsible, everyone agreed that. It was part of being perfect.

'Good girl,' said her mother, kissed them both, and was gone.

Beth looked at her little sister, already unzipping a banana. How could anyone eat so much, she wondered, and yet remain so very small? Juliet seemed to have been the same size for ever. It wasn't fair.

'Do you really want toast?' she asked.

'Yes please,' said Juliet, so Beth in her boots walked cautiously across the kitchen and put two slices of bread in the toaster. The boots felt wonderful. The slight tightness around the toes was pleasant, not painful. She decided she would wear them every day.

'Peanut butter or jam on your toast?' she asked Juliet.

'Both. Please.' Juliet was now in the middle of a handstand against the kitchen door.

'Both? Are you sure?'

Juliet came down from her handstand, swallowed half a pint of milk in four gulps and nodded her head speechlessly.

'Ok, both then,' agreed Beth. 'I don't know why you don't burst. I'm sorry about the boots though. Maybe you should ask for some yourself on your next birthday. No good waiting for mine; you'd probably have to hang on for years . . .'

Beth paused to reassess the feeling in her feet again

and found it was still fine. Wonderful, in fact, she decided, then was suddenly struck by a very happy idea. Which was that if her boots were still all right, then maybe other things were too. Perhaps it was just some diabolical trick of photography that had made her friends' heads seem only to come up to the height of her ears. Maybe all her worrying had been for nothing. Maybe Treacle . . . (after all, he had been properly clipped for summer for the first time for ages) . . . maybe Treacle just *looked* smaller. In comparison to how he had looked unclipped.

Once Beth had thought of it, she had to know.

'I'm just going out for a few minutes,' she told Juliet hurriedly. 'Just to see Treacle . . .'

'Be-ee-ee-th!' moaned Juliet.

'There's time if I run . . .'

'You'll make us late!

'I won't. You've still got all that toast to eat. I'll be back before you're finished.'

Beth grabbed an apple and some bread (nobody ever went to visit Treacle empty-handed) and fled before Juliet could protest any more. She did not have far to go; just along the lane that ran beside their house, past the allotments, and there was the little field they rented, with the corrugated iron stable-shed, and Treacle himself, standing by the hawthorn hedge and curling his lip to make terrible faces at the goats who lived next door.

'Treacle! Treacle!' called Beth, as she climbed the gate.

He heard at once, and came running, nearly knocking her over in his anxiety to see what she had brought him.

'Oh, you are greedy!' exclaimed Beth, hanging on to the gatepost so that she did not get tumbled on to the wet grass by the gate. 'Let me look at you! Stand still, I can only stay a moment!'

She gave him his apple and he nudged her lovingly, dribbling apple crumbs down her front. Beth pressed her face into his neck to sniff his sweet pony smell. Although he was supposed to belong as much to Juliet as he did to herself, it was Beth who rode him and brushed him, scrubbed out his water tub and cleaned out his shed. Juliet would never do anything like that. Nor would she ride him.

'Sitting on animals,' said Juliet, 'is just not me!'

Sometimes Juliet would keep Beth company in the stable while she forked and shovelled and brushed out corners, but she would never offer to help.

'I don't like poo,' said Juliet.

Treacle finished his apple and began gobbling brown bread. He ate with his forehead rubbing against Beth's hand, chewing and scratching at the same time. Beth looked at him with love. She had had him since she was eight years old and had needed to climb on the top of the gate to get on to his back. Now, admitted Beth, as he plundered her pockets, it was much easier.

It took just the smallest of hops . . .

All summer long, uncomfortable facts had been growing more and more clear to Beth. The fact that owning Treacle was expensive: 'The plutocrat', her father called the farrier, and 'I paid for that,' her mother had recently remarked, stuck in traffic in her ten-year-old car behind the vet's purring Porsche. That was one fact.

Another was that Treacle had been bought for the girls to share, and Juliet was not sharing.

'It's not good for him to be ridden by just one person,' said Beth, visiting her sister at bedtime one night in the hope of making her understand. 'He'll get lazy.'

'Take him to the riding school then,' said Juliet. 'Lots of people would ride him there. They need more ponies. They've got a waiting list because they haven't enough.'

'How do you know that?'

'I know a girl who goes there,' said Juliet, picking up a foot and putting it behind an ear without seeming to notice she'd done it. 'She told me. She said they're buying more soon. I bet they'd buy Treacle if you wanted. Shall I ask her to ask them?'

'NO!' cried Beth. 'All I said was, he needs more riding. That's all!'

'Ride him yourself then,' said Juliet, and she picked up her other foot, wedged it behind her other ear, and added, 'Easy.'

Easy, thought Beth unhappily.

It wasn't easy. That smallest of hops was followed by the hardest facts of all. The immense height from which she seemed to look down on to Treacle's neck. The way her feet when out of the stirrups could brush the seed heads of the long autumn grasses. The memory of Juliet's hilarity the last time she had watched Treacle and Beth canter across the field.

'What's so funny?' Beth had demanded.

'Only that you look just like you're riding a bike,' said awful Juliet. 'It's your knees! It's because you've grown so much!'

'I won't grow any more,' vowed Beth, desperate in her boots. 'I won't. I won't. I won't.'

Chapter 6
The Road to School

Alison, Ruby, Caddy and Beth usually met up at the crossroads and walked to school together, unless Alison was feeling particularly antisocial and decided to stalk off on her own. This morning things were different though. This morning it was Ruby who set off alone.

'I need time to think,' she told herself.

Ever since she had begun school, Ruby had been happy. First at her primary school, and then even more at secondary school. She had been there for a year now, and she loved it, which none of her friends could completely understand. Alison could not see why anyone would like school at all, but Caddy could feel the charm of the welcoming, battered, chewing-gum-speckled buildings, although she didn't like school work, lesson after relentless lesson, with hardly a pause in between.

Beth liked the fact that at school she was not expected to be perfect or even particularly sensible, but she minded the vast amount of time it took out of her life, whole weeks vanishing while Treacle was alone in his field.

But Ruby loved it, especially in company of Caddy and Alison and Beth. Away from those three she was a timid person, but with them around her she was as brave as a lion. No subject could frighten her, no homework was too long, nor any lesson too difficult. In fact, thought Ruby, they were not difficult enough, she could never quite see why her friends toiled and groaned and needed so many explanations to get through the day. Maths for Ruby was a series of puzzles, each more ingenious and revealing than the last. Languages, she absorbed as familiarly and easily as if she had heard them spoken in her dreams. Science and history and geography sent her racing to the library in order to discover more. Technology was bliss to her three-dimensional mind.

Ruby had been perfectly content at school until the day at the end of the last summer term, when she had torn open the brown envelope containing her report, and read what they had to say about her, with Caddy reading over her shoulder.

Now, walking to school, she recalled that afternoon. Here was the drain, down which she had poked the fragments of that fatal document. How foolish she had been, not to guess that they kept copies! How unresourceful, not to have supplied a fake!

Ruby had a problem and she had a solution to the problem that was so awful she could hardly believe there was no alternative. She wondered if it was actually possible.

'You can do anything you set your mind to,' her grandparents were always telling her.

I'm setting my mind, thought Ruby grimly, as she marched along the road to school.

Alison was the only one waiting at the crossroads that first morning.

'*Ruby's* sneaked off without us,' she informed Caddy, as Caddy came racing up to meet her. '*Beth* rang me a minute ago to say we're to explain that she's going to be very, very late. *And what's the matter with you?*'

'Me?' Caddy asked. 'What is the matter with me?'

'You look awful,' said Alison. 'Awful! That's what!'

Alison herself looked wonderful. She had put on purple lip gloss, eyeliner and mascara, rolled the top of her skirt so that what was left was hardly visible beneath her untucked blouse, and tied her tie (fortunately also purple) round her forehead like Pocahontas. Her nails were so newly varnished they were still slightly tacky and her long fair hair had been straightened and trimmed with nail scissors to make a ragged fringe that covered one eye. Even her school bag was gorgeous: shiny black with a design of tear drops in silver. It was a spectacular effort, especially considering that the first moment any member of staff spotted her she would be handed a baby wipe for her face, a black elastic band for her hair, and a copy of the school's standard leaflet entitled *Preparing for Your Working Day*. (It included step-by-step diagram instructions on *How to Tie Your Tie*, as well as *Six New Ways to Learn* and *Have Fun*.) Within ten minutes Alison would look exactly like everyone else (but grumpier). It would all be wasted. She was doomed.

But for the moment, she was perfect. It cheered Caddy up just to see her. She said admiringly, 'You look completely fantastic, Alison!'

Alison sniffed in a pleased kind of way.

'What happened to you?' she asked, and her glance took in every detail of Caddy's knotty bunches of hair, overflowing school bag, scuffed black ballet shoes and bare legs.

'Oh, things,' said Caddy.

'You got up early enough to get ready. I saw your light on.'

'I know, but we forgot it was school.'

'*Forgot it was school!*'

'Mmm. 'Til Indy reminded Dad.'

'Has your dad come home again, then?'

Caddy nodded, and Alison looked knowing. It was well understood among Caddy's friends that when her father came home it usually meant things were not tranquil in the Casson house.

'He came back yesterday,' said Caddy, and paused because she found that she could not bear to recall the reason that Bill had come home so suddenly.

Alison glanced at her, realised something was wrong, and did her very best to make Caddy feel better.

'Want to borrow my lip gloss?'

'Oh!' exclaimed Caddy, hugely touched. 'Oh yes, oh thank you, Alison!'

''S'OK. And I've got a spare comb. Sort out your hair while I pack your bag. Go on. It's nice, your hair. It'd take any colour dye!'

'Would it?'

'You should think about it. A really good pink, maybe. Or purple.'

'It's not allowed,' said Caddy. 'It's in the school rules. *No recreational colours!*' she added, quoting from the prospectus.

'That's so pathetic!' said Alison. 'Why'd they think the colour of your hair has anything to do with them?'

'I don't know.'

'They're all control freaks,' said Alison. 'It's a sign of

insecurity. Borrow my body spray, then you'll be all right.'

There was something very comforting about being with Alison, thought Caddy. It was like an escape, just to hurry along beside her, listening to her opinions on everything she passed. With every step, the troubles of the night were left a little further behind, and it seemed to Caddy that if only they could go on walking and walking, further and further, they would reach a point when they were gone completely, and the world was itself again.

They were in sight of the school gates now. There was the crossing patrol lady, enemy of the bus drivers. There were the bus drivers, tearing their hair. There were a thousand variations on school uniform, not one alike, nor one like the illustrations in *Preparing for Your Working Day*.

'Look, we've got new litter bins!' exclaimed Caddy, cheering up more and more as the world of school began to envelop her. 'Purple, how posh!'

'You sound like you're glad to be back,' commented Alison.

'Aren't you, Alison, even a bit?'

'I hate it,' said Alison, calmly. ' I hate every brick in the walls. Every window, every door. Every lesson, every classroom, every book, every rule. All the staff and all the kids . . .'

'No, you don't! You don't hate me! Or Ruby, or Beth! Oh there's Dingbat! Dingbat! Dingbat!'

'Aren't you over that idiot Dingbat yet?' demanded Alison, disapprovingly, but Caddy, who wasn't, had gone.

Chapter 7
Dingbat

Dingbat, a year older than Caddy, Beth, Ruby and Alison, had captured the hearts of the girls one by one, starting with Caddy the term before. He had arrived at the school as an unexpected new boy, gazed thoughtfully around the foyer, spotted Caddy, lolloped over, and remarked, 'I like your hair. It's just like mine!' and smiled his cheerful Dingbat smile.

If he said anything else, Caddy did not hear it. She was completely dazzled. For Caddy, time had stopped. Nor could she reply. '*Mine . . . Mine . . . Mine*' echoed Dingbat's voice in her head, over and over, like the ringing of a gong.

'Say something!' said Dingbat, and his grin widened as he pushed a tawny curl back from his face.

'Oh!' said Caddy. 'Oh, I can't believe you noticed me! That's amazing! Wow!'

★ ★ ★

'Talk about obvious!' said the scandalised Alison afterwards. 'You practically fell down at his feet!'

'Yes I did,' said Caddy.

'Without even knowing one thing about him!'

'What does that matter?'

'Staring at him as if you'd been struck by lightning!'

'I couldn't help it.'

'Oh, Caddy, wake up!' complained Alison. 'He's not that special!'

Her words sailed past like words in a dream. For Caddy, Dingbat was more than special. In those first few days she wouldn't have been surprised to notice that he trailed a comet train of stars.

She was like someone unexpectedly handed a fortune they hadn't known they needed. She clutched it, astonished and grateful, and could not think how she had managed to live without it.

So that was that: Caddy and Dingbat, sorted.

Almost.

As far as Caddy was concerned, after Dingbat's arrival, every other boy in the world could have been whisked off to a parallel universe and she would not have noticed. But for Dingbat things were otherwise. Dingbat had restless, adventurous eyes. They were always on the lookout for the next good thing.

'I'm just going over to say hello to Beth,' he

announced, about a week after his lightning strike, when his comet trail of stars was still as bright as ever. 'You don't mind?'

At that small but ominous question a little chill ran down Caddy's spine, because why would she mind Dingbat saying hello to Beth, unless . . . unless it was a particularly significant hello. Was it? Was it? Caddy wondered, and if it was, what then?

Could Beth be expected to withstand that which had so lately knocked herself, Caddy, off her feet?

Then Caddy was inspired.

'Mind?' she asked. 'Beth's lovely. Of course I don't mind. In fact, I think we ought to share!'

'*Share?*' repeated Dingbat, very taken aback.

'You and me and Beth!'

'*Both of you?*'

'Mmmm. Yes.'

'*Would she?*'

'Ask her,' said Caddy bravely.

That was how Dingbat came to be shared. He got used to it very quickly. He had always liked being appreciated, and he had always been the sort of person who, when offered a box of chocolates, took two.

Or even three.

'Hi, Ruby!' said Dingbat, and his green eyes sparkled, three-cornered and half closed, like a happy dog's.

'I think it's nice not to leave Ruby out,' said Beth. She was fond of Dingbat, but it was Treacle's photograph that decorated the cover of her jotter. Nor did she feel the need to write all over it: *Dingbat Dingbat*, in curly beautiful letters all decorated with stars.

That was Caddy.

Alison was full of scorn when she heard that all three of her friends were going out with the same person.

'Not that you do go actually out!' she said. 'You don't do anything, hardly! Save him a place in the dinner queue and write his name in fancy letters! That's it, just about!'

'I took him on my sponsored walk for Donkey Rescue!' said Beth indignantly.

'I did all his ICT homework!' said Ruby. 'All of it! I got rid of the stuff he'd tried to do himself and made him a whole new presentation!'

'He's babysitted Saffy and Indigo with me twice now,' said Caddy.

'Call that going out?' derided Alison. 'I bet none of you have snogged him properly!'

'Alison!' they all exclaimed, very shocked indeed.

'Ha!' grinned Alison. 'I knew you hadn't!' and she became quite amiable.

Sharing Dingbat went on all summer, and when the new term began nothing much had changed.

Perhaps fewer stars in the comet trail, but that was all.

Dingbat smiled his lovely, pleased-with-himself smile and looked often at Alison.

'Alison,' Caddy, Beth and Ruby explained apologetically, 'hates everyone.'

'I know, but not me!' said Dingbat, and despite no encouragement from Alison he persisted in this belief. Four out of four he wanted, Alison, Caddy and Ruby and Beth.

And especially Alison, because she always said no.

Chapter 8
Awful Day

Beth developed a way of walking that involved no movement of the bones of her feet. Sitting down, she felt no pain at all. But at lunchtime, in the dining hall, measuring the steps to the water cooler and deciding she was not thirsty after all, she became more and more preoccupied. The boots were agony. The afternoon classes were timetabled for the science block, and the science block was a long way away.

'What's up?' demanded Dingbat, sitting down beside her.

'My boots feel awful.'

'Take 'em off.'

'I can't. I haven't anything else to wear. I forgot my PE shoes.'

'You could try lost property. There might be something there you could borrow.'

'I've already looked, but there were none that

fitted. I've got weird feet,' muttered Beth, crimson with shame.

'They look fine to me,' said Dingbat, peering under the table.

'Yes, but they're . . . they're . . . eights.'

'Eights!' said Dingbat, much too loudly. 'Whew! Huge! I'll check out boys' lost property for you, shall I? I bet you only looked in girls'.'

Beth opened her mouth to protest.

'Don't say no!' ordered Dingbat, and vanished.

He was back before Beth's agony of blushes had faded, carrying a pair of unspeakable black trainers with knotted unmatching laces. He flourished them proudly above his head as he crossed the dining hall to Beth.

'Eights!' he called for all the world to hear. 'Perfect! Just like mine!'

'Oh, Ding,' moaned Beth, but all the same she dragged off her boots and put on the trainers while Dingbat watched approvingly. He could see nothing embarrassing about the situation at all, in fact, if he could have chosen a shoe size for Beth it would have been eight.

'Just like mine!' was Dingbat's ultimate compliment. 'Don't say no!' was his habitual command. Not that many people ever did say no to the cheerful Dingbat. Or that he would have taken any notice of them if they did.

Now he grinned at Beth (already puzzling over the problem of getting through the rest of the day without anyone seeing her feet) and asked, 'Alison about?'

'She's over there,' said Beth, nodding to where Alison sat on the far side of the room, scribbling urgently on a small piece of paper.

'She's dead stubborn, isn't she?' remarked Dingbat, waving in Alison's direction, and being ignored as usual. 'She's had all summer now, to get used to the idea.'

'What idea?'

'Me. Why's she looking so angry?'

'She's in an awful mood,' explained Beth. 'She's writing a letter of complaint to the school governors. She thinks she's being victimised. She's got detention already.'

'Seriously cool!' said Dingbat, sauntered across the room to the corner where Alison sat, and asked, 'All right if I sit here? Don't say no!'

'No!' snapped Alison.

'Mind if I read your letter?'

'Yes I do!'

'Just thought I'd say if you need any locker space, I've a little bit left.'

Alison snorted.

'I love your handwriting. It's just like mine.'

Alison slammed her things together in a heap and began pushing them into her school bag.

'Don't go! Wait a bit! I came across to see you specially!'

'I knew this was going to be an awful day!'

'Ali! Ali! Ali! That's not very nice!'

'Wasn't meant to be,' snapped Alison, because the thing that Dingbat must never know was how much she liked curling tawny hair. And wicked green eyes. And the appeal of ruthless complacency combined with a wide happy smile. And most of all, he must never know that if Caddy and Ruby and Beth ever grew tired of him . . .

Alison shoved that thought to the back of her mind and shoved Dingbat's grabbing hand with a very sharp elbow.

'Who do you want to go out with then,' asked Dingbat, all loud and cheerful, 'if you don't want to go out with me?'

Alison left.

Ruby's awful day started early in the morning, first with her head of year, and then, after her tears had subsided to self-pitying sniffs, with the head of school. The results of her last school report had begun. Such spectacular levels as she had achieved in every subject, the hard work that she had obviously put into her last year's studies ('I didn't!' cried Ruby, at this accusation, 'I didn't work hard at all!') not forgetting her end-of-term English essay (which had turned into ten thousand witty words on the private thoughts of Queen Victoria) all these innocent activities, now appeared to come with consequences attached. Moved away from all her friends, top sets in every subject. Timetabled to begin a second language (going into lessons with the year above) and member of the exclusive fast track class whose privileges included extra maths, extra science and Mandarin Chinese.

'But none of my friends do any of those things!' wailed Ruby.

'The Warbeck Scholarship becomes available at the end of this year,' said the Head. 'It is a very valuable award, and as you are aware, Ruby, you have been invited to apply. I for one am quite sure you will not be disappointed. We are all very proud of you.'

The Warbeck Scholarship had been the main subject of Ruby's school report, and its shadow had hung over her all summer. It was for a place at the private school in town, a girls' academy famous for its history of academic success, its beautiful grounds, its uniform of kilted skirts and immaculate blazers, and its efficiency in filing its students into the most inaccessible universities in the country.

'They offer a range of twenty-five "A" levels,' the Head told her wistfully. 'Things we cannot even dream of. Ecology and anthropology. Philosophy, Latin, archaeology now as well, I believe. Their science faculty is wonderful. There are visits to foreign language schools, field trips, visiting lecturers . . .'

'Why can't we have those things here?'

'We couldn't possibly afford it. I wish we could. To be absolutely honest, it's a struggle to maintain what we have. As it is our sixth form gets smaller every year. It's a wonderful chance for you, Ruby. You'll understand when you visit.'

The part of Ruby's brain that had thought *amazing* when she first read of the scholarship forced her to ask, 'Could Caddy and Beth and Alison come too?'

'There is one scholarship awarded per year available to us,' said the Head patiently. 'It is intended to cover fees, extras such a music lessons, school trips, uniform and equipment. It's value in money terms per year is approximately fifteen thousand pounds . . .'

'*Fifteen* . . . but . . . so does that mean not Caddy and Beth and Alison?'

'I think you know the answer to that as well as I do.'

'Then I'm not going to visit!' said Ruby, trembling.

'I won't do extra classes. You can put me in the fast track class but I won't be fast-tracked! You can't make me.'

'We'll talk again when you are a little more used to the idea,' said the Head, kindly. 'Meanwhile, I think you had better rejoin your class. Thank you for coming to see me, and telling me how you feel. I appreciate that.'

'It's no good being nice,' said Ruby, and she dropped her new homework diary into the Head's empty wastepaper bin and ran out of the room. She spent the rest of the school day on the top of a pile of exercise mats in the gym (having intelligently remembered that no one ever had gym lessons on the first day of term).

'Wasn't that really boring?' asked Beth as (once again in her excruciating boots) she limped home with her friends at the end of the day.

Ruby nodded. She had never known a day so long. She had calculated the number of seconds until the end of term, read a first aid manual, predicted the movement of shadows on the netball court outside the window and used a sturdy hair slide to take to pieces and reassemble the broken lock of the first aid cupboard door, and yet still found herself drowning in oceans of empty time.

'Are you planning to hide like that every day?' asked

Alison, and Beth said, 'You can't possibly. You'll have to come to classes, whether you like it or not.'

'What I'm going to do,' said Ruby, 'is nothing. Not listen. Not work. No homework. Nothing. I have to stop learning things.'

I have to stop growing, thought Beth.

I have to do detention tomorrow, thought Alison furiously. Again!

'I have to tell you something,' said Caddy, and then changed her mind, and added, 'not just now,' and walked along very carefully and quietly, reviewing the day in her head.

A very long day, and not over yet.

Beth left the group, and then Ruby. Alison turned towards her own front door.

Then they had all gone, and Caddy was home.

Chapter 9
The Firework Baby

Caddy's father was waiting for her outside the house, alternately tapping his watch and waving hurry-up signs, and breaking off every minute or so to rush to the car. It looked like he was having trouble keeping the doors closed. Inside Caddy could see Indigo and Saffron. They seemed to be bouncing off the roof and sides.

'Sit *down*!' ordered Bill, through the closed car window. 'Put your seat belts back on! Caddy, where on earth have you been?'

'Just school,' said Caddy.

'I expected you home half an hour ago! I . . .'

His voice was drowned out by a terrific banging, Saffy and Indigo, hammering on the windows.

'Stop that at once!' he roared in exasperation and they rolled on their backs laughing, and then began seeing whether they could touch the car roof with their toes. Their father gave a sigh of great weariness. It had been an exhausting business, just to meet them from school, walk them home, and organise them out of the house and into the car.

'You'd think you didn't want to go and see Mummy!' he had exclaimed, which surprised them very much.

'We DO!' said Saffron.

'We do,' echoed Indy. 'And the firework baby!'

It was true. They wanted to go very much. They were seething with excitement. Yet that seemed to make no difference to the efficiency with which they got ready. The job of getting them both into the bathroom, out of the bathroom, into their shoes and into the car had astonished poor Bill, and it had been nothing compared to the problem of keeping them there, once they were in. Indigo had needed a drink, and Saffron had forgotten the card she made at school. Then Indigo had wanted pencils and paper to very quickly make a card of his own. Also a rubber. A pencil sharpener. And felt pens. And no sooner had Indigo been equipped than Saffron's socks had begun to feel funny. She had pulled them off, posted them through the car window to her father and demanded other, normal-feeling ones instead. Not white. Nor stripy. Nor boys' ones. Nor the last pair that Bill produced which had Christmas puddings on and played a tune.

'Pink ballet socks,' said Saffron.

'But you don't do ballet!' protested her father, and Indigo spilled his drink and then Caddy came dreaming down the road and Bill lost his temper.

'Do you know how long we've been waiting here for you?' he demanded.

Caddy bent down to peer in the car.

'Why have you locked up Saffy and Indigo?' she asked, reaching for the door handle.

'*Don't* let them out!' roared Bill, pulling her away. 'They've been out about forty thousand times already! Just go into the house and get yourself sorted and we'll be off.'

'Off where?'

'Good Lord in Heaven! To the hospital, of course!'

'Oh.'

'So don't just stand there! Pop inside. Put something clean on. Get back out here as fast as you can.'

'I was going to have a sandwich. I usually do. We all do. After-school sandwiches.'

Bill squeezed his eyes tight shut and beat his forehead against the roof of the car. While he was doing this, Saffron (who had miraculously heard the word sandwich from inside and was suddenly famished) climbed over Indigo and succeeded in escaping by the front passenger seat door before her father had time to open his eyes.

'I want a sandwich too,' she said. 'So does Indy. We

can eat them while Caddy gets ready.'

'Right!' snapped Bill. 'I've had enough. Caddy, indoors, upstairs, come down clean! Saffy in the car! Indigo stay where you are! I am going into the kitchen and I will make sandwiches for anyone who manages to behave which will only be Indigo so far, because he is the only one not being an absolute pest.'

Saffron scrambled back into the car ordering peanut butter and jam.

'You'll have what you're given,' said Bill. 'That's a lovely picture, Indigo! What is it?'

'Oh,' said Indigo, looking suddenly absolutely heartbroken. 'Can't you tell?'

'Yes of course.'

'What then?'

Indigo's father, who hadn't a clue what his son had drawn, changed the subject very cleverly.

'How would you like,' he asked heartily, 'to look after the car keys for me while I make the sandwiches? Do you think you could manage that?'

Indigo, very bright-eyed, pushed aside his picture and nodded enthusiastically. Thankfully, Bill passed the car keys through the window and escaped, herding Caddy in front of him.

'Why'd you draw a swimming pool?' asked Saffron, inspecting Indigo's picture.

"'Tisn't,' said Indigo, climbing into the driving seat.

'Why's there a diving board then?'

"'S'not a diving board it's God,' said Indigo, flicking on first the radio, then the windscreen wipers, then the lights.

'God looks like an old man, not a diving board,' objected Saffron.

'It's not a diving board,' said Indigo, turning on the engine. 'It's steps . . .' he stood on the accelerator '. . . and that's God on the top of the steps.'

"'S'got his arms up to dive,' said Saffron very loudly over the roaring of the engine.

'Those are wings!' shouted Indigo, putting on the hazard lights and leaning on the horn, and then Bill ran out of the house swearing with his hands full of sandwiches and Caddy came after him and left the door open and didn't remember until they were halfway round the big roundabout on the other side of town.

'You three kids are beyond belief!' moaned Bill, as he headed back the way he had come, 'and now there's another one of you!'

'You don't sound very pleased,' commented Caddy. 'I knew you wouldn't be. I remember when Indigo and Saffron—'

'Caddy!' protested Bill, giving her a very pained look over his shoulder, and then said in a completely different

83

voice, 'Indigo, take your hand off the gear stick NOW!'

'Mummy lets me change gears for her,' said Indigo.

'I don't think that can be true.'

'She does,' said Saffron. 'She does me too. Else how'll we ever learn to drive?'

'Good Lord in Heaven!'

'That's what I drew,' said Indigo. 'What you say. Good Lord in Heaven . . .' He nodded forward suddenly, sighed, and fell asleep.

By the time they reached the hospital Saffron was also asleep. She and Indigo had to be shaken awake, guided groaning through the enormous car park and prodded along miles of corridors. Then suddenly their mother appeared, almost unrecognisable, with bruised-looking eyes, wobbly lipstick and a new dressing gown.

'Darlings!' she exclaimed.

Saffron screamed and hugged her as if she had not seen her for weeks. Indigo beamed and presented his card. Caddy said, 'Hi Mum,' and then found herself speechless.

Tears began, unromantically affecting (as they always seemed to do in the Casson family) noses more than eyes. Bill handed out tissues. A nurse hovered, raised her eyebrows at Bill and looked at a door labelled: WC.

Bill ordered hand washing for everyone.

This caused Indigo to lie on the floor and wail, 'But WHEN are we going to see the firework baby?' so pathetically that when they were clean again it was he who was first to be led into the special care baby unit where the latest member of the family had taken up residence.

He became perfectly quiet.

Saffron pulled away from Caddy and Bill to catch up. The watching nurse stopped hovering and walked purposefully after them.

Saffron was the next to see, and she made a noise like a gasp that was half indignation and half intense disappointment, as if Father Christmas had come and gone and taken the presents with him.

'Is that IT?' she demanded, turning to stare incredulously at her parents.

Eve gave a great sigh.

'Why's it look like that?' demanded Saffy. 'Why's it all tied up in a machine? Why's it not like a proper baby? Are you sure,' she asked the nurse, glaring through suspicious, half-closed eyes, 'That's not somebody else's?'

'Quite sure,' said the nurse, smiling with a lot of very white teeth.

'What a SWIZZ!'

'Untie it!' commanded Indigo.

'We can't do that just now,' said the nurse. 'All those lines and tubes and wires you see are what we use with very small babies. They need them to help them breathe and feed, and monitor their hearts . . . listen!'

The baby was making a sound. A wheezing cry, so like the sound that the late Lost Property had made that Caddy winced to hear it.

'Isn't that cute?' asked the nurse.

Indigo, still speechless, looked up at her as if she was insane. Saffron, deep in shock, said, 'It's AWFUL!'

'Saffron!' moaned Bill.

'AWFUL!'

Indigo nodded mournfully.

'Of course she's not awful,' said Eve. 'She's wonderful! She's going to be wonderful! Look at her tiny hands!'

They were purple claws, waxy and ancient-looking.

'Awful,' said Saffron. 'She's hairy too. Hairy shoulders even! That's a bit yuk!'

Bill moved forward and grabbed. Saffron suddenly found herself out in the corridor.

Indigo could not bear it. He sniffed and wiped his nose on his sleeve, then his eyes, and then his nose again. His sleeve began to look damp.

'What is it, Indy?' asked Eve, holding him in a gentle hug.

'Babies don't look like that.'

86

'Very small ones do.'

'Let's just unplug all that stuff and get her out of that box and go home and not come back.'

'We will, one day.'

'Now.'

'Not now.'

'Else would she die?' asked Indigo in much too loud a voice, and then he too was magically teleported to the corridor.

'I have never been so ashamed,' Caddy heard her father say, and Saffy's voice, very stroppy, 'Let go! I don't like it here . . . Indy, come on!' and running footsteps, three sets, two escaping, one in pursuit.

Caddy wished with all her heart that she too could run away. Nothing she had imagined in the past summer was as bad as this reality. The arrivals of Indigo and Saffron now seemed trivial in comparison. This baby, this calamity, that Eve thought so wonderful, was an impossibility. No need to fear, as she had earlier in the summer, that it would come home and drive her father even further into the distance with its wails. This baby would not come home. It was the human equivalent of her poor fallen baby bird, as helpless and hideous and doomed.

Even its cry was the fledgling's cry.

Caddy reached for Eve's hand and took a deep breath

(because what would happen to her mother when the inevitable came about if she was not warned from the start?) and began bravely, 'Mummy. Remember Lost Property?'

'Mmmm?' said Eve, bending over her fledgling.

'And how you said you knew, right from the beginning . . .'

'Caddy darling, this is a baby!' said Eve, laughing a little.

'Knew from the beginning he just couldn't . . . And it was horrible when he died, and I had tried so hard. Awful. Because I had got so fond of him.'

Eve was humming very softly. She said, 'Look, Caddy, she knows my voice. See how her breathing changes when I sing.'

'It doesn't really,' said Caddy. 'I thought Lost Property knew his name, but he didn't really. I just wanted him to.'

'I think her hair is going to be dark, like Indigo.'

'I thought Lost Property was growing feathers!' said Caddy. 'Can't you see? She hasn't GOT any hair.'

'When the light is behind her you can see she has very fine, dark, silky hair,' said Eve, patiently but insanely. 'A little bit wavy too.'

'Mum!' groaned Caddy.

It was no good. It was hopeless. Eve would not listen.

She said, 'We'll have to find her a wonderful name.'

The baby wailed again its heart-tugging wheezing cry.

'Poor little thing!' said Caddy. 'You can see it's in pain! It's miserable! Can't they do anything?'

'They can do lots of things when she's a bit stronger,' said Eve. 'Don't look so forlorn, Caddy darling, please.'

'Can I touch her hand?'

'Of course you can.'

For a moment Caddy's finger stroked a mottled purple fist. It felt hardly warm, hardly alive, but it did something strange to Caddy. It made her tremble with fear. Hurriedly in her mind, she began the familiar reviewing of her assets, preparatory to the usual bargains with God. That was no use. She was overspent already that summer. She could think of nothing she had not offered for the life of Lost Property.

'What can I do?' she asked hopelessly.

'You don't have to do anything,' said her mother, hugging her. 'Just be Caddy. Can I hear the others coming back?'

She could. Bill and Saffy and Indigo reappeared at the door, and Caddy was thankful to see them. Even the horrible scene that followed, when Saffron realised that Eve had no plans to abandon the baby and come home and light fireworks was a relief.

'But Daddy PROMISED!' shouted Saffron. 'PROMISED! This morning! Before breakfast! Didn't he, Indy?'

'He promised,' agreed Indigo.

'Eve darling,' said Bill earnestly. 'I swear I didn't . . .'

'You sweared about me driving the car,' interrupted Indigo.

'. . . say a word about bloody . . .'

'Swears a lot,' said Saffy vindictively.

'. . . fireworks. I shouldn't have brought them . . .'

'Bloody shouldn't,' agreed Saffron.

'I'm taking them home. They're tired. Everyone's tired.'

'I'm not bloody tired,' said Saffron, but all the same after a kiss from Eve she was hauled away.

'About bloody time,' said Saffron.

Caddy was glad to go too. Only Indigo darted back into the baby room for one last look at the thing that had caused so much trouble.

'Get better!' he whispered. 'Getbettergetbetter!' and dashed away.

Chapter 10
The News

During the next few days, as the arrival of the new baby became general knowledge, cards and flowers began to appear at the Casson house. Not many flowers, but a lot of cards. Some said 'Congratulations'. More said, 'Thinking of you'. One or two remarked that the family were in their prayers.

'What a cheek!' exclaimed Caddy, who did not like the idea of being prayed for, willy-nilly, whether she needed it or not.

Another person suggested that the children might like to start putting together a memory book.

'What's a memory book?' asked Saffron suspiciously, because it sounded like homework.

Indigo, surprisingly, knew the answer to that. His class at school had made a memory book for a classmate who was going away.

'But no one's going away,' said Bill firmly, and after

that he began checking the insides of cards before he allowed them on public view.

Beth's mother was more practical. She appeared with a large lasagne which even Saffron consented to eat. Ruby's grandparents sent round a lot of back copies of *National Geographic* and a chocolate cake with a dip in the middle. Alison's mother produced a beautiful arrangement of fruit (which pleased Bill) and the unfortunate remark that it was lucky he was able to take so much time off work so easily (which didn't).

Away from home things were different. Caddy, once Ruby, Alison and Beth knew the bare facts, said, 'I'd rather not talk about it. At home, it's the only thing.'

That was all right, until school heard the news. Someone had a parent who cleaned at the hospital. Rumours began of possible death and probable brain damage.

Caddy became very upset.

Alison imposed a news blackout on the subject of babies, explaining that she was perfectly willing to pull off the heads of anyone who did not comply.

This worked.

Everyone returned to their own preoccupations, except for Beth's mother, who sent round two more lasagnes before she ran out of dishes to send them in.

Then she stopped too.

And that was the end of the news.

Chapter 11
What the Normans Ate

Beth had a good idea. It came to her at school, during history, when the history teacher announced to her unelectrified class that for the first half of term they would be doing the Normans.

'We've done them!' moaned the class on hearing this news, and as if to prove it people added, "We did them ages ago in Year 6!' 'We did the Normans the same term that we did growing-our-own-beans-and-carrots only it didn't work!' 'The term we did nothing in art but draw the same chair!' 'The term we had three supply teachers because our real one had stress!'

Everyone, it seemed, in all their various junior schools, had done the Normans so thoroughly that they never wanted to hear of them again. And yet, when questioned by the history teacher, no one could remember a single thing about them, so mixed up were they in their minds with beans and carrots and chairs and other unhistorical things. Not even Ruby could (or would) contribute a clue to their existence. And this despite the fact that she had been taken all the way to France to see the Bayeaux tapestry, had walked its entire length, and had the postcards to prove it. Nothing relevant to the Normans could the history teacher prod from the class until a pale thin boy, with much smirking, at last put up his hand and announced, 'They had very small doors.'

It was the very small doors that gave Beth her good idea, because she knew it was true: she had seen them. Or one, anyway. There was a church in the centre of the town that, sooner or later, every schoolchild in the area was taken to visit. It had Saxon foundations, Elizabethan carvings, Victorian windows, a crypt so full of mildew and the aroma of old graves that it caught in the throat, and a Norman doorway.

The Norman doorway was so small that it fitted ten-year-olds better than teachers (who had to duck). Nor was it built especially for Norman ten-year-olds, school children were told, class after class, year after year, generation after generation going back goodness knows how long, almost as far as the Normans perhaps. Not at all: it was a full-sized adult door. People were smaller then. Healthy. Healthy enough to conquer England, for instance, which no one had managed since.

But smaller.

They ate much less.

If I was a Norman, thought Beth, I would probably not get any taller than the height I am now. I'd be thinner too, if I was a Norman . . .

Norman breakfast was easy. Only Juliet was there to notice what Beth ate, and she herself was far too busy eating to see what anyone else consumed. Norman lunch was no problem either: just a matter of eating the apple and passing the sandwiches to whoever held out a hungry hand. Even Norman supper, with the family altogether, was not too hard. You could say 'I had toast after school,' without saying how much toast. Or: 'I thought it was better to have an enormous breakfast and a very big lunch and less at night,' without actually eating the breakfast or the lunch.

'So it is,' agreed Beth's mother, about the breakfast and the lunch, and smiled at Beth, who (unlike her little sister) could always be trusted to be sensible.

However, it was hard being a Norman, meal after hungry meal. Very soon Beth, who in the past had hardly thought about food at all until it arrived on her plate, found herself thinking of it all the time. Also her sense of smell developed so wonderfully that she could smell when Juliet took the lid off the biscuit tin, she knew if there were bananas in the fruit bowl before she looked, and actual cooking became such a torment that she had to go out and visit Treacle when it was happening.

Even visiting Treacle was not without its problems. Pony nuts, Beth discovered, smelled deliciously sweet to those on a Norman diet. So did hay. Sometimes Beth chewed a little hay, when things were bad. However, sticking a photograph of Treacle on the fridge door helped a lot. So did drinking lots of water. So did chewing gum, in fact, chewing anything. And Juliet. Juliet helped, just by being her usual self.

Juliet did not forget the boots.

'Why have you stopped wearing them?' she demanded.

'They got a bit hot.'

'Not on me, they didn't. For me they were nice and cool.'

'Oh.'

'So can I borrow them?'

'No.'

It was suppertime. Their father was away, but their mother was there. She had made lovely vegetable soup and apple pancakes. Beth ate the soup but not the vegetables, and the apple but not the pancakes.

'Someone brought in chocolate brownies because it

was their birthday,' she explained. 'They were huge ones, with marshmallows on top.'

'Oh!' exclaimed Juliet enviously. 'Were there any left over?'

'Yes, loads.'

'What happened to them?'

'She shared them out again until they were all gone. Dingbat had three.'

'Three!' squeaked Juliet, pouring golden syrup on her pancakes. 'Three! Beth, you pig! If there were that many spare why didn't you bring some home for me?'

'Juliet, that's enough syrup and don't be a pest!' said their mother. 'And Beth didn't say she had three! At least I hope you didn't, Beth!'

'Of course I didn't,' said Beth, who, thanks to the useful Dingbat, had eaten none at all. 'And how could I have brought them home for you, Juliet? They were someone else's special birthday brownies.'

'You could have said, "Please could I have one for my little sister?"' said Juliet, grumpily stabbing her fourth pancake in its middle. '"Please could I have one or two?" you could've said. And then they could've said, "Of course, take all these if she'd like them," and you could've said, "Thanks, I'll bring the box back when it's empty . . ." What's the matter? Stop laughing, both of you! Anyway,' added Juliet (still not forgetting the boots) 'what I was saying was, if I can't have your boots just to borrow (how mean) can I have something else instead? Can I come to your room and do trying on to see what you've grown out of?'

'NO!' said Beth, but there were no locks on the bedroom doors and so Juliet came anyway.

'Go away!' ordered her sister.

'I'm just looking. Not touching,' said Juliet, opening the wardrobe door. 'At your old denim jacket that you haven't worn for ages. You must have grown out of that!'

'Well, I haven't.'

'Put it on and show me.'

Beth shut the wardrobe door so quickly Juliet only just snatched her fingers away in time.

'Your Snoopy slippers then! Look! They fit me perfectly.'

'Take them off!'

'Oh Beth, you hated them when Gran bought them.'

'I've got used to them now though,' said Beth. 'I know what I've grown out of that you can have though.'

'What? What?'

'All my Posy Pets,' said Beth, gathering up an armload of brightly-coloured, flower-spattered plastic puppies, kittens and rabbits.

'Oh, brilliant!'

'And my disco light!'

'Goody!'

'And my Tracy Beaker story CDs.'

'And the books as well?' asked Juliet greedily.

'Oh all right,' groaned Beth. 'The books as well! But that's all. And I won't be growing out of anything else for ages and ages, so don't ask!'

'I won't.'

'And no secret trying on either!'

'No, of course not, Beth,' said Juliet with such terrible sweetness that Beth took defensive action, emptied her school bag of books, and began repacking it with other things. The boots, Snoopy slippers and the denim jacket went in first, but other things were added too. Things that if Juliet appeared wearing would cause her parents to say, 'Goodness, Beth, have you already grown out of *that*?'

No one must notice her growing, Beth thought, and anyway, perhaps after a little while of eating like a Norman, those things would fit her again.

Juliet had not closed the bedroom door when she left. Beth could hear her in the kitchen, chattering as she displayed her loot to her mother.

'Oh, you are lucky,' she heard her mother say,

'to have a sister like Beth!'

'She's perfect,' agreed Juliet. 'It must be awful. I'm glad I'm not.'

Beth did not feel perfect. She felt tired, and slightly fragile, as if the easiest thing in the world to do would be to burst into tears, and the hardest thing afterwards would be to stop them.

From the kitchen her mother called, 'Like some hot choc, Beth? I'm making it for Jools.'

'Maybe later,' replied Beth, and heard her mother laugh and say, 'Of course! All those brownies! I forgot!'

Then the smell of hot chocolate began to billow through the house: great clouds of warm, sweet, chocolate-scented fog. It was too much for Beth. She pushed shut her bedroom door, flopped down on her bed, flat on her back, and let tears of self-pity trickle coldly down her cheeks and into her ears.

Juliet eyed the bedroom door speculatively as she came upstairs.

'What are you doing, Beth?' she demanded.

'History,' said Beth. 'Norman. Go away!'

Chapter 12
The Casson House

The Casson House had never been tidy. They were not a tidy family. For one thing, no one (except Bill) ever threw anything away. The rest of them were hoarders, and as a result there were things everywhere. Canvases for Eve's painting, piles of washed clothes, books, toys, half the contents of Grandfather's house because he was in a nursing home, more than half the contents of Eve's twin sister's Italian flat, sent home when she died. Also everything the children had ever brought home from school, or grown out of, or been given. If Treacle had been Caddy's pony there would have been no need to worry that one day he would be found a more suitable owner. He would have stayed for ever, like everything else.

'It's not exactly minimalist,' Dingbat had remarked on his first visit to Caddy's home, which had made Eve laugh and laugh, and like him very much.

It was surprising what one house could hold. When plays were put on at school teachers always asked the Casson children, 'Do you think your wonderful mother might be able to find us a long enough wig for Rapunzel? A Victorian birdcage? A camel? Cardboard would do, as long as it was big enough.'

Dingbat, who happened to be there when Indigo came home with the request for the camel, was very impressed that Eve (instead of shrieking with indignation as his own mother would have done) enquired, 'One hump, or two?'

'Like for the story,' explained Indigo.

'Which story?'

'How the camel got his hump.'

'Oh that story,' said Eve. 'There's one in the attic.'

'You've got a cardboard one-hump camel in the attic?' asked Dingbat incredulously.

'Mmmm. Propped up behind the Christmas trees.'

'How many Christmas trees?'

'Just a few from when Caddy's class did Narnia. They ended up here. I can't remember why. Do you think you and Caddy could help Indigo if he goes to look for it now? You might have to lift the rocking horse out of the way. And mind Grandad's cabinet. It's full of glass.'

Dingbat said he thought it was amazing the way the family knew where everything was. That made everyone collapse into astonished laughter, and Dingbat ask, 'What did I say? What did I say?'

'Darling it's not that we know where everything is,' Eve explained at last. 'It's more like we think we know where a lot of things might be.

'Which is good enough for us,' added Eve. She, Caddy, Indigo and Saffron lived amongst the clutter without hardly noticing it. It was just part of home to them, like the smell of drying paint and Eve's haphazard baking. Somehow it worked. People got to school more or less on time. Eve rushed out of the house to give art classes, home to paint pictures, up and down stairs to collect laundry, round the supermarket grabbing apples and bread and flowers and socks (because socks always vanished) and home again in time for everyone back from school. However chaotic the days, at the end of them nobody ever went to bed hungry, or unhugged, and always there was the possibility that Bill might come home, like the family's own private Father Christmas.

Bill coming home was always an event. He brought flowers too: florist flowers with ribbons and baskets. Exotic sweets appeared from his briefcase, theatre tickets from his pockets. For a day, or two, or three he whizzed them out of the house and away into the world, propelled by laughter and his own bright energy. For as long as Indigo and Saffron could remember, family life had been that way: their mother nearly always home, their father nearly always away.

Now everything was changed, and these changes were caused by the firework baby, who as the days went by, still continued to waver between the temptation of either causing chaos in everyone's lives by staying, or of wrecking everyone's lives by going.

The longer the firework baby stayed, the more excuses it seemed to find for leaving. It turned blue, and then yellow. It could not make up its mind to breathe unaided for any length of time. It showed no interest in opening its eyes. In the second week of its life it caught pneumonia and had to have antibiotics.

'That's not uncommon with very small babies,' Bill told the frightened Caddy as calmly as he could. 'A day or two, at the most, and everything will be fine.'

Saffron and Indigo looked at him sceptically. Those two would have made good spies. They had a sort of secret radar system that made them aware of things other people considered private. Their ability to absorb information from supposedly guarded sources was impressive and frightening. They lurked in the shadow of doorways, vanished among curtains, poked and pried, and became invisible behind the sofa during telephone calls.

Saffron and Indigo knew that, whatever their father

said, at the hospital people would be very surprised if the baby was fine in a day or two. When they were allowed to visit again (they were all banned at the slightest sniffle or tummy ache) they peered into the baby's plastic box and were amazed it was still there. 'Getbettergetbettergetbetter,' Indigo used to command, but the baby seemed so temporarily alive that he didn't really believe it would. Once, in the middle of the night, it stopped breathing completely, and alarms went off, loud alarms, calling for help.

'Stopped breathing!' wailed Caddy, also in the middle of the night.

'How did you know that?' demanded her father.

'Saffy and Indigo.'

Saffron and Indigo, inscrutably asleep, did not deny it, and neither did their father, but later he said to Eve, 'Caddy gets into such a state, I think it would be better if we did not mention . . .'

And Eve agreed.

Day after day, and then week after week, the baby endured, tied by tubes in its plastic box in the special ward in the hospital. And, except for the most fleeting visits home, Eve, who knew it heard every word she said, and recognised the names of its siblings in the stories she told, and preferred its yellow and pink hats to its blue and white ones, and already had dark curls and blue eyes and a precocious sense of rhythm, stayed with it.

So Bill took charge.

He began by throwing things away, starting in the kitchen, having long deplored the nature of Eve's catering.

'All my Coco Pops!' said Saffron indignantly. 'All the chocolate pudding mix! All the milkshakes!'

All the curry-flavoured instant noodles vanished as well. So did all the tinned spaghetti and microwave pancakes. Bill went shopping and returned with a great deal of salad, brown bread and . . .

'Porridge!' said Saffron in disgust, unpacking the bags while her father took one of his endless phone calls from London.

'Orange juice with bits in,' said Indigo mournfully. 'Yoghurt with bits in. Even the bread has bits in. I don't eat bits.'

'I've found something worse than that,' said Caddy.

'What?'

'Dead fish.'

'*What?*'

Caddy handed her package to Saffron who peered inside, screamed and threw it across the floor because it really was dead fish: rainbow trout, all complete with heads and tails.

'They've got faces!' whispered Indigo, horrified, and so they had. Faces with shocked open eyes and tragic smiles. By the time their father reappeared there were four new fish-sized graves in the garden, and three reproachful gravediggers in the kitchen.

Their father managed to laugh that time, and cooked them omelettes instead.

'With runny middles,' said Saffron.

'That's melted cheese.'

'Cheese and egg *mixed up*?' asked Indigo, and became very sick indeed.

'On purpose,' said Bill, unfair with crossness, and was attacked by Saffron and Caddy.

'I'm sorry, I'm sorry, I'm sorry!' he said. (He was never mean with apologies; in fact, no one did them better.) 'Poor sweethearts! Poor pets! Well done, Indigo! There's a brave chap! I've got the cure for this. I'll fetch it in a moment.'

The cure was wonderful cologne on a cool linen handkerchief. Bill folded it across Indigo's hot little forehead and Indigo got better.

'You should give some to the firework baby,' said Indigo, and Bill promised he would. He saw the firework baby much more often than they did because he went while they were at school. Saffron and Indigo grumbled about that, and said it was not fair. They grumbled on the days when they did go too, because their father demanded such high standards of cleanness and healthiness before he would agree to take them.

Caddy didn't complain however; the last thing she wanted to do was breathe germs on to the firework baby. At home she did her best to help, reading bedtime stories to Saffron and Indigo, unmuddling their school clothes, washing plates and dishes, and putting up with her father's attempts to reform them into a model family.

That was not easy. Bill seemed to be always getting cross, and although he was sorry almost at once, it didn't stop him snapping the next time someone made him annoyed. And, no matter how much Saffron protested, his cooking remained relentlessly healthy, and his habit of throwing things away that he considered rubbish, relentlessly ruthless. He took to insisting on early bed, even when the early bedded people lay awake for hours, not sleeping, and after the first week or so of school, he enrolled Saffron and Indigo into after-school club, so they didn't get home for ages and ages. His phone calls to London got longer too, and he shut the door when he made them so no one could hear what he said.

Caddy's school did not have an after-school club, and home, with its irritable new ruler and its closed doors and tidiness, was not a place she wanted to be. More than ever she clung to her friends, Alison, Ruby and Beth. Somehow, the genie did not seem to touch that world.

Caddy said, 'Let's make a promise to never, never change.'

'Let's,' agreed Ruby, and 'Perfect,' said Beth, but Alison laughed.

'Hmmm,' said Alison. 'I don't think so.'

Chapter 13
Somewhere to Go that isn't Home

One Friday afternoon near the end of September they all walked home from school together: Dingbat, Caddy, Ruby, and Beth, and even Alison (miraculously not in detention for the first time for days). Beth was slightly ahead of the group with Ruby. Glancing sideways, she stealthily measured her height against her friend's. She was almost sure that the difference was a little less. She knew that her school trousers were definitely looser. That was good. But bad was the weary feeling in her legs and wrists, and the way that thoughts of food ambushed her from every direction. Even a glimpse of the spire of St Matthew's in the distance made her swallow with hunger and turn to Ruby to ask, 'What did the Normans actually eat?'

Ruby was the perfect person for questions like that. She didn't demand, 'Why do you want to know?' because to Ruby wanting to know came naturally. She brightened up, although she had been rather quiet most of the way home, and said, 'Oh! The Normans. Let me think! Not potatoes of course, because they hadn't been discovered. Or tomatoes either. So no chips and sauce!' (Beth swallowed again.) 'Nothing very sweet, I don't suppose. No sugar cane, you see, probably only just honey for sweetness. No oranges or bananas or things like that. No chocolate, poor things! Nor tea or coffee or pasta, or rice or curry . . .'

'You're just telling me what they didn't eat!' objected Beth. 'Tell me what they did!'

'I think they grew wheat, so bread, I suppose. And things made with oats like porridge. Vegetables of course. Cabbages and things. Cheese if they had cows. Eggs if they had chickens. I bet there's books in the library that would tell you . . . we could go and look if you like . . . No, we couldn't . . .'

Ruby paused.

'Why not?'

'I've lost my library card. I forgot. And I don't want to go to the school library. Somebody might see me.'

Ruby sounded so forlorn that Beth reached out a friendly arm to hug her.

'I told my mum about the scholarship that they said you could get,' she mentioned.

'What did she say?'

'She said "How amazing! What a lucky, lucky, lucky girl!"'

Long ago, when Ruby had first heard of the scholarship, there had been a moment like the crackle of a spark. A cliff-edge tingle of thrill and panic. Until common sense combined with fear had saved her, pulled her back from the brink of the unknown and into the friendly world again.

Now, for a moment, Ruby found herself looking over the edge once more.

'Did you tell your mum I wasn't going to go?' she asked.

'Yes,' Beth nodded, 'and Juliet who was listening as usual (she listens to everything) said, "She's mad. I'd go." (Juliet's not afraid of anything),' explained Beth, apologetically.

'No,' agreed Ruby, and sighed. It had been terribly difficult that week, to sit through lesson after lesson showing never a flicker of interest. To ask no questions, and give no answers. To explain, without flinching, to teacher after teacher that she no longer did homework, not ever, for any reason, not even if they put her in detention (but they did not seem to put her in detention. They nodded, understandingly, as if they had been warned not to fuss). Ruby noticed their knowing smiles and felt uncomfortable, as if she had been caught cheating.

At home the uncomfortable, cheating feeling was even worse.

'Ruby, Ruby, Ruby, Ruby!' her four grandparents had greeted her on the first day of term. 'How was school?'

'Boring,' said the new, cheating, Ruby, slamming down her bag.

'What?' they demanded, astonished. 'All of it?'

'Yes. Useless. Every single class.'

'Every single class! Whatever were they? May we see your timetable?'

'I didn't bother to copy it down.'

'Didn't bother?' they asked, and a swift look of surprise passed between them. 'Well!'

'Loads of people don't bother copying it down,' said Ruby truthfully. 'They just ask their friends what's next.'

'What a happy-go-lucky approach!' said the grandparents. 'We must be getting old! Never mind! Any news of the Academy scholarship?'

'Oh that?' asked Ruby (still the awful new pretend Ruby) and nearly added, 'Don't think that's going to happen!'

Just in time Ruby came to her senses. It would do

no good making remarks like that, she realised. Not just because if she did the grandparents would immediately ask more questions, but also because it would make them very sad. Better, thought Ruby, who was very fond of her grandparents, to say as little as possible to worry them and then just quietly fail the scholarship at the end of the year. So she picked up her school bag, stooped to hug Wizard the cat and said, feeling much more like herself again, 'The beginning of term's always boring, you know.'

'Bound to be,' her grandparents agreed, sounding very relieved. 'It's always the same until things get up and running. They'll have things organised and your after-school clubs going soon.'

Ruby could have howled. She had forgotten the afternoon clubs. And how could she go to them, uncooperative non-student that she had now become? Chess Challenge. Eco Watchers. Page Turners, Drama Group and Science Team. There was one for every day of the week. That meant every day there would be an hour at least, when she was not expected at home and could not be at school

What'll I do? she wondered. When all those things start up again. What will I do with all those hours?

It soon became a problem. Ruby tried the town library, but that was no good. Quite apart from the fact that she had disposed of her library card, it nearly always contained at least one grandparent. She found herself playing hide and seek around the bookshelves and getting very odd looks from librarians.

Friends' houses were no use either. Beth's contained the inquisitive and persistent Juliet, always underfoot with questions and opinions. Alison's had never been welcoming. Caddy's had, until Caddy's father took charge, and then it became almost as bad as Alison's. Ruby had worried about the after-school hours for days, and still not found an answer. Now, walking home with Beth and Caddy, she spoke her problem aloud: 'I need somewhere to go that isn't home.'

Beth understood at once.

'So do I,' she said.

Caddy, who was tagging along, sometimes listening, sometimes lagging behind with Alison and Dingbat, was surprised to hear Beth say that.

'Why?' she asked.

Beth hesitated. She did not know how to explain that home, and especially the kitchen of home at the end of a hungry school day, was full of temptations greater than anything the Normans ever had to resist. Her Norman dieting was a private thing, and she had a very strong feeling that her friends would not approve.

'Because Juliet is such a pest?' guessed Ruby.

'She is a bit,' admitted Beth, glad of this explanation.

'But you've got somewhere to go, Beth,' said Caddy. 'Treacle's stable.'

'I know, but I can't go there. I have to go straight home to let Juliet in. I've got the house key, and if I'm even a minute or two late she acts like she's about to die of starvation on the doorstep. And then I'm supposed to keep an eye on her until Mum gets home.'

'What would she do if you didn't?'

'I don't suppose she'd do anything. She just watches telly and eats sandwiches. And crisps. And cereal and biscuits and apples and lumps of cheese. And bananas. And if there's anything left over in the fridge like cold roast potatoes, or sausages, or . . .'

Beth stopped abruptly, realising that her reply had turned into a menu.

'I'd rather be at Treacle's,' she said, pushing away her hungry thoughts for a moment. 'I worry about him being on his own so much. Only Juliet won't come. She's too lazy, and she says she's too hungry, and she's not allowed to eat in the stable because of germs.'

'Well, I know what!' said Caddy. 'We could all go back with you, and take turns to keep an eye on Juliet. You and me and Ruby and Alison. Then you needn't be there all the time, Beth. I should like a place to go that wasn't home as well, and Treacle's would be lovely.

117

And in between, I wouldn't mind watching Jools chew up apples and things, would you, Ruby?'

Ruby shook her head. It seemed a wonderful solution to her. 'It would be nice,' she said wistfully. 'We could bring things to read.'

'Would you really not mind helping with Jools?' asked Beth. 'Because if you wouldn't, it would be perfect. What about Alison?'

Alison was now far behind, sauntering along beside Dingbat, looking almost as if she was enjoying herself.

'We'll ask her when she catches up!' said Caddy. 'Look at poor old Dingbat! He's trying really hard!'

Dingbat had been trying really hard ever since they left school. All week he had been toiling to make Alison understand what she was missing. This afternoon he was showing how useful he could be, carrying the excess baggage of all his admirers: art projects, PE kits, lunch boxes and jackets. He bore his burdens well, more like a camel than a donkey, rising above them with no noticeable distress and a good deal of complacence. He swayed a little, but he did not stagger: in fact, he begged for more.

'Ali, Ali, Ali, Ali! I've got everyone else's junk! Why not let me take yours too?'

'In your dreams, Ding,' said Alison, quite amiably for Alison. 'Besides, you'd fall over.'

'Ali, come to the cinema tomorrow afternoon with me and the others,' said Dingbat. 'Come on, Ali! Say you will! Say you will!'

'I'd rather die,' said Alison. 'Saturday afternoon cinema is full of smelly little kids. Their mums dump them there while they go round the shops.'

'You can sit between Caddy and me. We'll protect you from the little kids!'

'And the floor is always knee deep in popcorn and drink cartons . . .'

'I'll clear you a little path and you needn't look down! Come on, Ali! We need you, Ali! You ask the others if you don't believe me. Oy! Caddy, Ruby, Beth!'

They turned round and waved, but then turned back, and became deep in conversation.

'They're scared you're going to make them carry their stuff,' said Alison.

'I wouldn't do that!' protested Dingbat. 'I've got it all balanced! Hey, you three, slow down!'

'They're going faster,' said Alison, laughing.

'Oh well, I don't care,' said Dingbat. 'Say you'll come tomorrow, Ali! I need you, Ali! I really do! Caddy is cute. And Ruby's amazing. She's brainy, just like me! And Beth is sweet! She's really special! But . . .'

'I'm glad you like my friends,' snapped Alison,

suddenly freezingly aloof.

'But what about gorgeous, Ali?' demanded Dingbat, refusing to be frozen, letting fall his burdens, spreading his arms wide, taking up the whole pavement. 'What about gorgeous, Ali? I haven't got a gorgeous, Ali! Not a totally, perfectly, gorgeous! Look! I've dropped everything for you!'

So he had. Jackets, bags and lunch boxes. Everything.

'That won't work,' said Alison, and jumped over everything and ran to catch up with Caddy and Ruby and Beth.

Caddy and her friends looked doubtfully back at Dingbat, all alone now.

'Is he all right?' wondered Beth.

'Who cares?' asked Alison.

'I'll go back and get our stuff,' said Caddy. 'Come with me, Ruby, Beth! And then we'll tell Alison about Treacle's!'

'Treacle's?' asked Alison, when they came panting back. 'What's so special about Treacle's?'

'Treacle's,' Caddy and Ruby and Beth explained, 'is just what we've been needing. Somewhere to go that isn't home.'

Chapter 14
Managing

Caddy said, 'When I have a house I won't bother with furniture from shops. I'll just have straw bales and hay bales in every room.'

'What?' asked Alison. 'A hay bathroom? A hay fridge? A hay cooker?'

'You can have hay cookers,' remarked Ruby. 'They're called hay boxes. There was an old book I read once, about some children who lived in a barn. They cooked in a hay box.'

'Did they use a hay loo?' enquired Alison.

'In old books people never go to the loo,' said Ruby, 'so probably not. Anyway, I only remember the hay box. I always wanted to try one out.'

'Not here!' said Beth hastily. 'You can get awful tummy bugs, eating in stables. We can't have food here. Not even biscuits or sweets or anything like that. Or crisps, or choc or sandwiches . . .'

'OK,' said Ruby, surprised at her intensity.

'Or fruit even, unless maybe an apple for Treacle. Or a carrot or two. He shouldn't really have bread, I'm going to stop bringing it for him except for a bit of brown sometimes. But . . .'

'Beth, we've got it!' interrupted Alison. 'No food! We've understood. Stop going on! Relax, and admire the furniture!'

'It is good,' admitted Beth. 'It smells lovely too.'

On Saturday afternoon they had abandoned Dingbat and the cinema plans, and spent the time transforming the storage half of Treacle's shed into a home. Now the corrugated iron walls were lined with golden straw bales, stacked like giant Lego blocks. Hay bales made sofas and chairs and beds, and even a hay bale dressing table for Alison. Ruby had a bookshelf that she filled immediately. Behind was a secret cupboard for Beth.

'I've got to have one place where Juliet doesn't come poking,' she said, explaining it to her friends.

'What do you need, Caddy?' they asked, when the dressing table and the bookshelf and the cupboard were complete.

'I just need to be here,' said Caddy. 'It feels safe here.'

'Safe from what?'

Safe from the genie, thought Caddy.

The last week at home had been awful. There had been
a trip to the hospital, when Eve, wild-eyed from lack of
sleep, seemed to have forgotten the outside world. She
had asked, 'Are you managing?' and 'Caddy, are you
managing?' and 'What about Saffron and Indigo? Are
they really managing?' and said, 'I spend the nights
wondering, how are they all managing . . .'

'Eve! For goodness' sake!' Bill snapped at last.

'Be nice to my mummy!' Indigo had said, turning
on him with a fury that shocked them all.

'I apologise, Eve,' Bill told her humbly. 'I'm
very tired.'

Eve said of course he was, no wonder. 'Poor darling
daddy,' she said, with her arms around Indigo, and
then got out her sketch book and showed them
pictures she had drawn of the baby in the plastic box.
They were drawings of a baby not visible to anyone but
Eve, with dark eyes, and curly toes and no need for
tubes and monitors and masks to ensure that it did not
forget to breathe.

Saffy said, 'They're pretend pictures.'

'They're lovely,' said Caddy.

'Lovely,' echoed Indigo, but he looked at them, and
then at the hunched and ancient original very

doubtfully and turned away.

'They'll be good for if she gets dead,' said Saffron cheerfully. 'Because then we'll forget what she really looked like and we can pretend they are true.'

'Thank you, Saffron,' said Bill, and marched off to the coffee machine down the corridor.

'Daddy,' said Saffron, 'is in a very, very, very big mood! Isn't he, Indy?'

'Don't tell Mummy that!' said Indigo.

'Because of his London lady . . .'

'Oh yes!' cried Indigo, suddenly happy. 'Yes, tell Mummy that!'

'I am!' Saffron began to speak very quickly, her eyes on the door in case her father came back. 'Daddy is in a very big mood because yesterday Caddy answered the phone and it was his friend from London. That London lady, who always telephones. And she said, "Please can I speak to Bill Casson?" and Caddy said, "Yes, I'll fetch him," and she went to fetch him so I had the phone and I said, "You might have to wait a very long time," and she said, "Oh dear, why would that be?" and I said, "Because I know where he is." So then she said, "Then could you fetch him please?" and I said "No." So she got very ratty and said, "Where on earth is the man?" and I said, "He's in the bathroom doing splashers." "What?" she said. So I said, "Splashers!" *What?*" she said, so I shouted, "SPLASHERS!" and then suddenly she said, "OH! That's all I needed to know," and she didn't stay any longer and Daddy said, "Good Lord in Heaven knows how much that call cost me. I can never look her in the face again," and it's not fair because now he won't let any of us answer the phone . . .'

'But,' interrupted Indigo, who was suddenly flat on his back on the floor, prostrated by laughter, 'it's really good Mummy, because when one of us says, "Where's Daddy?" (and someone is always saying "Where's Daddy?") the other one says, "He's in the bathroom doin' . . . doin' . . ." you say it, Saffy!'

'Splashers!' shrieked Saffron, collapsing into such giggles on top of him, that even Caddy and Eve had to join in.

'What's the joke?' demanded Bill, returning with the coffee. Luckily he could not understand the words that Saffron and Indigo hiccuped from the floor, and Eve was too kind to enlighten him, while Caddy was too wary. She knew her father's patience with the inanities of little children had almost completely run out.

Saffron and Indigo, limp with silliness, took a lot of getting home that afternoon. By the time they were there, Bill was cross again.

I ought to help more, thought Caddy, in bed that night. The trouble was, helping aggravated Bill so much. Whatever Caddy did, vacuuming, or tidying-things-under-sofa, or (her favourite job) scooping out the velvet-soft ashes from beneath the grate of the fire, her father would appear and say plaintively, "Caddy darling, the dust! The noise! And really, is this the right *time*?' When, to cut down on dust, Caddy tried vacuuming the ashes from the grate, and vacuumed up a still hot ember, things became very bad indeed. The ember had smouldered for hours in the vacuum cleaner bag while everyone was out. Caddy's father came home to find all the smoke alarms going off and a hideous smell of hot plastic. 'No more cleaning, thank you, Caddy,' he had told her very firmly.

'I could cook then,' she offered. 'I can cook. Eggs and pasta and things.'

'That's a very sweet offer,' said Bill, busy on the phone to John Lewis, ordering a new vacuum cleaner.

'So shall I then?'

'Suppose you leave it to your poor old dad? Eggs and pasta! I think I can manage something a bit more exciting than that.'

'But eggs and pasta keep you alive,' pointed out Caddy. 'They'd do! Saffron and Indigo would eat them!'

'They'd get scurvy,' said Bill.

'They could have orange juice.'

'Caddy, Caddy, Caddy, you never give up!' said her father.

'I help Mum,' said Caddy.

'Mummy's different,' said Bill.

She certainly was. She did not own any cashmere jumpers for one thing. Caddy accidentally added one to the armload of grubby socks and school uniform she scooped up from beside Saffron and Indigo's beds and piled in the washing machine. The socks and things came out beautifully but the jumper . . .

'Was cashmere,' said Bill. 'Was,' and dropped it in the bin with the vacuum cleaner.

'I think,' he told Caddy, 'we should each of us stick to doing the things we do best.'

'What do you think I do best?' asked Caddy.

'Look pretty,' said her father, and Caddy, who loved him so much, nevertheless found herself behaving very badly indeed. Sloshing plates and cups about recklessly in the sink. Rinsing them with floods of cold water. Dropping them in handfuls on the draining board. Slamming out of the kitchen leaving the plug hole blocked with tea bags and the tap running as hard as possible.

'Mopping the bloody floor again?' enquired Saffron, when she came in a minute later.

'Yes thank you, Saffron.'

'When we have sore throats Mummy gives us hot lemon with honey in it,' said Saffron. 'It makes you better.'

'It sounds lovely.'

'So could I have some now?'

'Why?'

'I've got a sore throat.'

'Are you sure you don't just want hot lemon and honey? You can have that without making up a sore throat, you know.'

Saffron sneezed and wiped her nose on her wrist.

'Saffy!' exclaimed her father, turning round in surprise. 'Was that a real sneeze? Let me look at you! Tell me about this sore throat.'

'It's sore. But not like Indigo's. Indigo says his throat is itchy.'

'Good Lord in Heaven!'

'And his ears ache,' said Saffron, and sneezed again, and it was a proper sneeze, because this, her father realised, was a proper cold. The swollen-nosed, long-lasting, infectious kind that goes on and on.

'Everyone at school has got it,' said Indigo. 'Even my teacher.'

Bill put Saffron and Indigo to bed with hot lemon, hot-water bottles, earache medicine, and four chapters of Lemony Snicket read aloud with no complaining because he felt so guilty about doubting Saffron's sore throat.

Once they were in, his thoughts became wild. Of what happened to children with colds at boarding school. Of boarding school, and how in principle he did not believe in it, and how much it would cost anyway. Of hospitals, where sore throats and earaches were not welcome. Of all he could be doing in London, if he was in London. Of how on earth he would occupy Saffron and Indigo, all the time they would be home.

In all Bill's wild thoughts, never once did he think of doing what Eve would have done, which was to stuff the invalids' pockets with paper handkerchiefs and send them to school to sneeze in company with all the other sufferers. The next morning, to their great delight, he kept them home. There he gave them a lesson in hand washing and not spreading germs, checked their temperatures, dosed them with vitamins, listened to Indigo read three pages of his reading book, dragged Saffron (squirming and complaining) through ten lines of hers, found them an education channel on TV, and disappeared with his laptop to the lair he had made for himself in a corner of the big bedroom upstairs.

'If we are poorly enough to stay off school we ought to have medicine,' said Saffron.

'Cough medicine,' agreed Indigo, who had had some

once before and never forgotten the delicious burnt cherry taste of it.

'Yes, cough medicine,' agreed Saffron, fetched Bill's latest bottle of red wine (opened out of habit but hardly touched because he never knew when he would have to find his car keys and drive to the hospital) and poured a dose for herself and another for Indigo.

'Lovely, lovely,' said Indigo. 'More!'

'No, you'll get drunk,' said Saffron bossily. 'Now we'll do music with Caddy's recorder.'

Entirely by ear, and with no reference to conventional fingering, they took it in turns to improvise long discordant tunes, pausing only to shake out the spit now and then. They discovered an ear-numbing screech that could only be produced with high pressure blowing and competed to see how long each could make it last. Now and then Bill shouted beseechingly from his lair, but they took no notice until he came down, removed the instrument of torture and suggested lunch. He made them neat triangular cheese sandwiches, produced orange juice and yoghurt, and obligingly helped drape tablecloths to turn the table into a cave. They furnished it with bears and cushions and lay around snoring.

'Lunch,' said Bill, but they did not seem to want to eat until he went back to his lair. Then Indigo looked very thoughtfully at the orange juice, hunted out a sieve and sieved out the bits.

'Indy!' exclaimed Saffron admiringly. 'How clever! Can you do the yoghurt too?'

'After I've cooked the sandwiches.'

'*Cooked* them?'

'Mmmm. Cooked will be better for our colds.' Indigo opened a tin of beans, poured them into a saucepan, balanced the sandwiches on top, and turned on the heat. The beans bubbled, the cheese in the sandwiches turned to goo, and the bread went beautifully orange and soggy. Jubilantly Indigo scooped his creation on to two plates.

'I didn't know you could cook, Indy,' said Saffron, quite overwhelmed.

They ate with spoons and reverence, licked their plates bare and prudently washed the saucepan and put it away. Sieved yoghurt was not such a success though. However much they poked it, it stubbornly refused to pour through the sieve.

'Never mind,' said Indigo, the new family cook. 'We'll turn it into trifle.'

The simple addition of smashed-up biscuits turned the yoghurt into trifle. Saffron, who only the evening before had refused to eat ham because she could see the edges, and fresh pineapple because she never had before, scraped up the pinkish-grey gunge with gusto, and asked, 'What'll we do next?'

'If we had anything dead we could dig graves with square corners,' said Indigo.

Hopefully they hunted first through the garden, and then through the fridge, but without any success. Evidently whatever frightfulness their father planned to perpetrate in the way of supper that evening had been very well concealed. In the end they had to settle for the most worn-out-looking bear in the cave. That was Old Panda, who over the years had become so badly unstitched under his chin that his head was half off.

'So he must be dead,' said Saffron. 'Anyone would be.'

Old Panda's funeral took most of the afternoon, and Old Panda's exhumation after Indigo woke up hysterical at one in the morning seemed to take most of the night. Locating the grave, by fading battery torchlight, was almost impossible. Bill unearthed more than one dead fish before he hit the right spot. He refused to let anyone help with the digging and ordered them to bed. Saffron and Caddy watched the shadowy figure in the garden from their bedroom window, but Indigo took the opportunity to give himself a few more doses of cough medicine. Bill caught him merrily glugging down the last one, and was not pleased. Saffron and Caddy had to rush down to defend their little brother, which they did by shouting a lot, and slamming doors.

The last traces of Bill's patience vanished at half-past three in the morning. Caddy was asleep on the sofa and Indigo (snoring happily) had been carried upstairs, but Saffron was still wide awake. She stood over her father, beady-eyed and critical, refusing to go to bed until he sewed on Old Panda's head.

'Ouch!' said her father, stabbing himself.

'Are you bleeding?' demanded Saffron. 'Don't drip on Old Panda if you are.'

Bill put down Old Panda, picked up Saffron, removed her muddy shoes and, gripping her firmly by the ankles so she couldn't kick, carried her up to bed.

'Go to sleep *instantly*,' he ordered and went back down to post Old Panda into the washing machine, and then to finish what was left of Indigo's medicine. Caddy woke up just as Old Panda began to bubble, and her father took his first sip.

'What if you have to drive to the hospital?' she asked sleepily. 'Suddenly. Because it's an emergency. What would you do?'

'Taxi,' said Bill. 'So don't worry! We're still managing aren't we, Caddy? More or less?'

'Yes,' agreed Caddy, as she fell back asleep to the sound of Old Panda's churning. 'I suppose we are. Managing. More or less.'

Chapter 15
Important Tuesday

Old Panda had been removed from his grave on a Monday night, four weeks exactly after the frightening Monday night when the firework baby was born. Tuesday was an important day for him: the start of a new life with a securely attached head.

It was an important day for other people too. It was the day that Ruby read the Academy prospectus, and Beth discovered Mars bars. Also the day that Alison's life began to change. And the day that the firework baby had been waiting for.

On that morning Ruby had a large white envelope in the post: an invitation to spend a day at the Academy. There was a school prospectus in with the invitation, deliciously fat and glossy, full of lists and pictures and articles and maps, so exactly the sort of thing that Ruby liked to read that it might have been written with her in mind. It made her feel trembly to look at it.

'Something interesting?' enquired a grandparent, who had seen the envelope but not the contents. 'Or just the usual junk mail?'

'Just junk,' said Ruby, and stuffed it hastily in her school bag out of sight.

On the same morning, on her way out to work, Beth's mother paused to look at Beth and remarked, 'You never seem to take Treacle to the riding stables any more.'

Beth stared at her in surprise. It was true, she didn't, although she had hardly noticed it herself.

'You used to like going,' persisted her mother. 'You did those courses, didn't you? Jumping and cross-country riding and pony first aid. Shouldn't you like to do something like that again?'

'Oh,' began Beth. 'I don't know . . . I hadn't thought . . .'

'Bethy, are you worrying about money?' asked her mother. 'Yes, you are! I knew there was something wrong! You needn't, darling! And anyway, Gran was asking only a day or two ago what on earth she could get you for your birthday. She suggested something like that, since, as she said, the only thing you really care about is that pony! Beth? Bethy darling . . . ?'

Because Beth was staring at her in complete astonishment. Money? Who was worrying about money? Not she, Beth. In all her many worries that particular trouble had never shown its horrible face. What she was worrying about, and the unacknowledged reason she had not been to the stables for so many months, was that there she would be bound to encounter some horsey and tactless person who would take one look at herself and Treacle and say, 'Goodness Beth, you are getting very big for that little pony!' All in an instant, Beth realised that. Also in that instant, another fact became clear: if she was not worrying about money, then her mother certainly was.

'What were you saying about money?' Beth asked.

'Nothing, nothing that matters at all,' said her mother reassuringly, knowing, as she did, what an infectious worry money was when it got loose in a family. 'Oh dear! Oh, don't look so surprised! Promise me, Bethy, I just thought . . . I should never have said a word because actually we are managing very well. Very well indeed! And I have those extra hours now too . . . so!' And then Beth's mother had kissed Beth and rushed off to work, eager to do those extra hours.

Like people were, when they were worrying about money.

Beth sniffed a bit, as she set off for school that

morning, trudging behind in Juliet's exuberant wake. The trouble with a Norman diet was it left you constantly on the verge of tears. Were the Normans always in floods? wondered Beth. Did they snivel a bit as they buckled on their miniature suits of armour, or measured out their tiny doorways? Did they drip and hunt for hankies as they marched towards Hastings in 1066? Were their Norman breakfasts sufficient to fortify them against such lapses? Beth doubted it. Her own Norman breakfast had left her weak with self-pity. Toast, one slice, with Marmite, one scrape.

At least I must be very cheap to feed, thought Beth, remembering her mother's anxious face that morning. Not that her mother would be pleased at her Norman efforts, Beth knew. Furious, probably, would be how she would feel. It was very lucky indeed that Juliet was as unNorman in appetite as a person could possibly be. Juliet ensured that the right amount of food disappeared from the breakfast table; her breakfast of Sugar Puffs (most of a family-size box), chocolate spread (half a jar) dug out with a spoon and spread on bananas (three) nicely balanced Beth's naked slice of toast.

Remembering Juliet's banana-bulging cheeks made Beth feel worse than ever. There was her sister, stuffed as a cushion, far ahead cheeking the lollipop lady. And here was she, starving.

Starving right beside the sweet shop that cunningly opened every morning just in time to part scholars from their dinner money and diets.

For one minute Beth disappeared from the pavement. When she reappeared it was with a Mars bar in each pocket and another in her hand.

The first went in three bites and three painful gulps. The second was almost as fast. She was gnawing the third as she hurried down the road to catch up with Juliet, swallowing the last traces as she caught her up, swaying by the time she reached school, dreadfully sick the moment she made it to the girls' bathroom.

'Did you have breakfast?' they asked in the office, as she lay on the sickroom couch, pale and clammy.

'Yes. Toast.'

'Just toast?'

'And three Mars bars on the way to school.'

'Three Mars bars!' they said. 'Serves you right!'

Beth stayed on the sickroom couch until 11 o'clock when she was issued with the standard emergency school breakfast for the faint and hungry (two Weetabix, one carton of orange juice, one cereal bar (optional)). Having consumed this feast and survived its consumption, she was issued with a sick bag (just in case) and sent back to class.

★ ★ ★

'Today,' said Alison's mother, 'is an important day for me.' She had begun cleaning the house at dawn. By the time Alison left for school she had reached the vacuuming stage. She shadowed Alison down the stairs, vacuuming her footprints off each tread. It looked like a show house. In the bathroom not even a toothbrush was visible as a sign that anyone actually lived there. In the kitchen all traces of cooking and eating were completely removed. Outside, the garden looked more than ever like a dolls' house garden. The lawn was newly mown, and over the weekend the flower beds had been planted with winter pansies, purple, white and yellow, mathematically placed.

'It's a pity about next door,' said Alison's mother, and she glared disapprovingly at the Casson house windows, with their bright, mismatched curtains, and the Casson house garden, all trampled grass and new-dug graves.

'Is it a pity?' asked Alison.

'It's none of my business, but I would very much like to know what was going on last night out there. Or did you sleep through all the noise and lights?'

'No.'

'Of course they're artistic,' said Alison's mother, and she said it a bit wistfully, knowing she wasn't. 'And She always smiles . . . I don't know about Him.'

'Everyone likes Caddy,' said Alison, looking across at Caddy's friendly window.

'You'd make new friends.'

'Hmmm,' said Alison, not at all enthusiastic about that idea. 'I might. Or I might not bother.'

'A fresh start in a different school . . . just what you need.'

'School is school,' said Alison, with loathing.

'It might be much better.'

'It couldn't be much worse,' agreed Alison. 'Nag, nag, nag! Moan, moan, moan! *"Alison, you are part of a community here!" "Alison, we shall have to contact your parents again!"* Last week this dismal old hag in a sack said, *"Alison, what makes you think we should alter our very high standards to accommodate you?"* So I said, "Stand beside me looking into a mirror and say that. And anyway, what makes you think I should lower *my* very high standards to accommodate *you?"* '

'Alison!'

'I'd done my eyes in four colours and she made me take every bit off before she let me into the dining hall! She guarded the door. You'll probably get a letter about it. Don't worry though. I've thought of a revenge!'

'I hope you haven't!'

'Wait and see then!' said Alison, and ran off to school before her mother could ask any more questions.

★ ★ ★

After all the excitement of the night before, the Casson family found it hard to get up that Tuesday morning. Caddy was the only one to go to school on time. Her father woke up enough to see her off, but then, despite having planned to spend a day of wonderful efficiency, he fell asleep beside the telephone. Saffron and Indigo discovered him there two hours later when they came down hunting for breakfast.

'Only it's nearly lunchtime,' said Saffron. 'What'll we have? Cereal?'

'Boring,' said Indigo, and searched through the kitchen. 'Rice pudding,' he announced. 'With jam. Pie thing I found in the fridge. Daddy's special cheese.'

'Daddy's cheese is mouldy,' objected Saffron.

'It's lovely mould. It tastes like bubble bath. I tried a bit.'

Saffron tried a bit too, her first taste of Stilton. It did taste of bubble bath; it was very nice. So was the rice pudding, made purple with blackcurrant jam. So was the pie thing, despite being laced with yucky asparagus and poisonous olives.

'We can pick them out,' said Indigo, but in the end they ate them.

'Your cooking is much better than Daddy's,' said Saffron.

'I know. Poor Daddy.'

They looked at him compassionately for a moment, and then dismissed him from their thoughts.

'What'll we do?'

'I'm going to school,' said Indigo.

'Are you?'

'Well, I'm not poorly any more. I had all that medicine and it made me better. Are you poorly still?'

'No,' admitted Saffron.

'Come on then. School.'

'What about Daddy?'

Indigo wrote a note:

Dere Daddy SAFFRON AND ME.
Are gone. To. sssSSss K hool.
love Indigo xxx and Saffron x

They laid it by his hand, and tiptoed out of the house.

'Ought we to lock the door?' wondered Indigo.

'No.'

'What if there's burglars?'

'They wouldn't want Daddy.'

A few minutes later the ringing of the telephone (on which Bill's unshaven cheek lay pillowed) nearly frightened him to death.

'Darling!' said a voice when he groaned into the receiver.

'Eve!' said Bill, after a pause for thought so long that his wife was alarmed.

'Are you all right?' she asked. 'Are the children all right?'

For a moment Bill (still dim with sleep) nearly said, 'What children?' which would have been disastrous, but then instead he heard himself repeat, 'All right?'

'Caddy? I worry about Caddy. I sit here and think, it's all too much for Caddy . . .'

'Caddy's fine,' said Bill as heartily as he could. 'Off to school, bright and early . . . do you think she's academic?'

Eve didn't. He could hear her shaking her head down the phone.

'Well she must be something,' continued Bill. 'It isn't art and she's not practical, far from it . . . Saffy and Indigo . . .' Bill looked around desperately ' . . . Saff and Indy . . .'

(Where were they? The house was silent, and when he looked outside, the garden empty.) 'Saffron and Indigo . . .'

Indigo's note caught his eye and he pounced on it, like a starving man on a sandwich. For a moment the randomly scattered, enormous lettering baffled him completely. He read forwards and then backwards with increasing bewilderment. Blinking, he thumped his forehead with his fist to help him understand, deciphered a word, found another, understood, and announced brightly, 'Saffy and Indigo are at school! So, nothing to worry about there. Now, your turn! Any news?'

'Yes! They're doing it today! Bill? Bill?'

Eve's voice suddenly sounded far away and panicky, like she was falling slowly down a well. That was just emotion, Bill knew, and best ignored, like Saffron's bad language. So he said, as coolly as possible, 'Are we talking heart surgery?'

'They've explained everything very carefully,' said Eve (still in her well-shaft voice), 'and they know it's not ideal, but I trust them absolutely. They're wonderful. It's wonderful news really. It's what we've been waiting for, after all. There's some forms to sign . . .'

'I'm on my way,' said Bill. 'Give me an hour . . .' (he glanced around the kitchen, at the mud and scattered food, at his own unwashed reflection, at Old Panda starfished urgently against the washing machine door) '. . . or so . . .'

'Or so,' sighed Eve from the bottom of the well.

'Superb,' said Bill. 'Excellent. Fantastic. Great news. Well done!'

★ ★ ★

Eve sang Happy Birthday to the fledgling, now one month old and more hideous than ever but clearly (noticed Eve) very pleased that the date had been remembered.

After Happy Birthday came The Reading of the Colour Chart, a rainbow document from a firm of artists' suppliers, usually kept on the kitchen wall. Eve had unpinned it during her last hurried visit home (hugs, shower, collapse on sofa, more hugs, sleep, grabbing of random items, tears, return).

The colour chart was no random item however, it was a vital part of the family's world. Caddy's and Indigo's names had both been chosen from it. Cadmium Gold for her glowing brightness (for months after Caddy was born, Eve was certain she radiated light, like an angel in a picture), Indigo for his wondering, shadowy, indigo eyes. Saffron also had a colour for a name, a spicy warm yellow. Now it was the baby's turn, and Eve read the names of the colours aloud, emeralds and violets, scarlet and perylene, siennas and magenta, ultramarine from beyond the sea, cerulean blue of heavenly skies.

The baby in its nest of tubes and wires listened impassively, waiting for its day to begin.

Chapter 16
At Treacle's

'How did we manage without Treacle's?' asked Caddy.

'It was always here,' said Beth.

'Not like this,' said Caddy, looking around, and Beth had to agree with that. Now the hay bale prickles were softened with throws, crimson and sage green, lent by Beth's kind-hearted mother. The colours looked good with the green and gold of the hay. So did the fan of feathery autumn grasses that Caddy put in the window, and the rainbow-makers she hung from the roof struts. They had music too, a CD player discarded by Alison and mended by Ruby. 'It just needed a new contact in the battery bit,' said Ruby. 'And a spring to keep the cover shut, I used one from a pen. The radio's working again too. It was only the aerial that needed fixing.'

'You are clever, Ruby,' said everyone, impressed.

Once the CD player was mended, anyone could tell who had arrived first by the music that was playing.

Friday I'm in Love was Alison's song. 'They are very Alison words,' agreed Ruby, listening carefully. Her own favourite *Puff the Magic Dragon* brought Treacle cantering across from wherever he happened to be grazing. Robbie Williams, to everyone's glee, sent him off in a huff to sulk.

At Treacle's they laughed more than they did in other places.

'Meet you at Treacle's!'

That was what they told each other every morning as they entered the school gates. Quite often they did not see each other much after that. Ruby would be hauled off to endure her extra classes. Alison spent a great deal of time in some sort of disgrace. Beth tightened her belt and drooped in quiet corners. Lately she had supplemented the Norman diet so heavily with Mars bars that Juliet (surreptitiously trying on her school jacket to see if it fitted her yet) wept with greed and indignation when she discovered the pockets full of wrappers.

'Beth!' said her mother reproachfully, when presented with the evidence (flung on the kitchen table with shrieks of 'It's not fair!'). 'I noticed you weren't eating properly yesterday! Is that what your pocket money goes on? I thought I could trust you better than that. I didn't even know you liked Mars bars!'

Beth didn't, they made her sick. Juliet did though. 'You'll get spots!' she told her sister revengefully.

'I won't. And anyway, Ruby says spots from chocolate is just a myth. She read it somewhere.'

'Ruby,' said Juliet, 'is boring. You're a greedy pig. Caddy is a mess. I don't like any of her clothes. Alison hates me.'

'Alison hates everyone. It's not just you.'

'It shouldn't be me because I don't hate her. I think she's cool. Cooler than the rest of you. Why didn't she come yesterday?'

'She was probably in detention.'

'I'm going to be always in detention when I'm grown up,' said Juliet admiringly. 'You won't catch me hanging round in a shed! Gobbling Mars bars and sucking my thumb!'

Ruby was the thumb sucker. She did it without thinking, especially when she was worried. 'Tell me when I'm doing it,' she begged, 'and I'll stop.' She didn't do it often because she was happy at Treacle's. Helping her friends race through their homework. Speculating on spiders and sunlight, the fragrance of hay, the movement of dust motes. Nothing was too small or too common not to interest Ruby. 'There are stories about dust,' she said, gazing at the sparkling haze in a sunbeam. 'I'm not surprised. Who do you think first thought of hay? Why does the smell of grass change when it dries? Spiders, if you think about it, must be able to hope. Or else they couldn't make traps. Did you know that the colours you see aren't the colours things are? They're the colour things reflect.'

'Really?' asked Alison, interested for once. 'I never knew that! That might be useful! Are you sure it's true?'

'Yes it's true. Well, it's obvious when you think about it,' said Ruby, to whom many things were obvious that baffled normal people.

Alison opened her mouth as if she would like to ask more, but Ruby was deep in her book again. She devoured books in Treacle's shed, making up for the hungry hours at school. She also pored over the prospectus of the Academy, usually in private, hidden among the covers of more respectable literature, but once with Caddy who was a good listener.

'Look, this is where I'm not going,' she said. 'Imagine if I did! Imagine if, all on my own, I had to go up those steps and through That Door one day!'

'It's only a door,' said Caddy laughing, but Ruby didn't laugh.

'You go through that door, and you're into that corridor. It leads to the hall one way and the cloakrooms the other. Look! There's a floor plan! Up those stairs, that's where the library is, but all the laboratories are round the back so you can't see them from the road. Imagine me in that uniform, talking to girls like those! I wouldn't know what to say! Look at the list of what they do in PE! Orienteering! I've never heard of anyone doing orienteering! And that's their clubs. "Clubs and Societies", it says. They've got a geology club, even, but anyway, I wouldn't know anyone in it.'

'Is geology fossils?'

'That's part of it. I bet they go on field trips. Here's photos of all the staff.'

'I know that one,' said Caddy, pointing, and added most surprisingly, 'She lives down the road from me and Alison.'

'Down your road?' asked Ruby incredulously.

'Mmm. The posh end.'

'I knew she'd be posh. Posh and scary.'

'She's got a little girl who has to have a wheelchair.'

'Why?'

'Why what?'

'Why does she have to have a wheelchair?'

'Because of her legs, I suppose,' said Caddy.

'Has she broken them? Did she have an accident? Is it something curable?'

'It can't be,' said Caddy logically, 'or else she'd get cured, wouldn't she?'

'We can make new joints,' said Ruby. 'We're beginning to be able to grow new nerves back . . .'

'We?' quoted Alison, eyebrows raised, but Ruby didn't notice. She had gone quiet, thinking.

There was lots of quiet at Treacle's, more than any other place Caddy knew. Quietness and friendliness. You could catch up on your dozing, or marvel at Ruby's brains, or watch as Alison sat at her hay dressing table, painting her eyelids in magical colours.

'Have a go?' offered Alison, and Caddy was soon peering from under rainbows of silver, yellow and purple. Beth and Ruby looked at her dubiously and refused to try themselves. They did not have Caddy's ability to enter so freely into other people's worlds. Still, they were glad to share their own with her. Often Ruby pushed a book or magazine towards her, saying 'Read this!' Beth measured her thoughtfully with her eyes and said, 'Perhaps I could teach you to ride. Yes. You'd be all right. Come and try.'

Caddie liked that idea, and followed Beth outside. They captured Treacle with carrots and flattery and hoisted Caddy into the saddle. No sooner had she got there however, than an unlucky and rare thing happened. Two horses came trotting down the lane that ran across the end of the field. Treacle, who rarely met his own kind any more, and had long ago exhausted the charms of goats, gave a squeal of pleasure and hurtled towards them. Caddy, with equal speed, shot backwards over his tail and landed on the base of her spine in the mud.

'I knew that would happen,' remarked Juliet, who happened to witness the accident.

'No, you didn't!' snapped Beth. 'Caddy, are you all right? You should really get on and try again.'

'OUCH! OUCH! OUCH!' groaned Caddy, rolling in agony. 'I can't! I couldn't possibly! I've broken all my bones right up to my teeth!'

'See!' said Juliet. 'I always said it wasn't safe! Shall I telephone an ambulance?'

Caddy shook her head, rolled on to all fours, and then with Beth's help, managed to stand, and then to stumble into the stable and drape herself face downward on a hay bale. After a while she recovered enough to stagger outside again, but it was a relief when Treacle refused to allow himself to be caught.

'He knows he's been naughty,' said Beth. 'He didn't mean it though, Caddy.'

'He was just excited to see those horses,' agreed Caddy. 'He probably gets lonely, here on his own.'

Beth's stricken face made her wish she could unsay those words as soon as she had spoken. 'I didn't mean that how it came out,' she said hastily. 'He couldn't really be lonely, not with all of us. I just meant . . . I don't know what I meant. My back hurts so I'm not thinking properly.'

'Do you think you should go home?' asked Beth worriedly.

Caddy shook her head and said that she'd rather be here, with her friends, than anywhere else in the world. Sitting down was still painful, so she helped Beth to shake out Treacle's straw in his half of the shed, arranged the throws on the hay bales in the other, swept the floor, tidied Ruby's books, measured out pony nuts and scrubbed Treacle's water tub.

'Why has he only got a cold tap?' demanded Alison.

'He's a horse,' said Caddy reasonably.

'Doesn't he ever wash?'

'You don't wash ponies, you brush them,' said Beth. 'I wash his mane and tail sometimes, though.'

'How?'

'With pony shampoo.'

'I didn't mean that,' said Alison. 'I meant how, with only cold water?'

'Oh,' said Beth, understanding. 'I fetch warm from the house in a bucket.'

'A *clean* bucket?' asked Alison.

'Of course,' said Beth, and showed Alison the very clean bucket that she used for shampooing Treacle. Alison scrutinised it inside and out.

'I suppose it would do,' she admitted, and on Friday she astonished them all by plonking a small cardboard box on the hay dressing table.

'Pink,' she said.

'What!' they asked.

'I can't do it at home because Mum would go mad if I got pink splashed in the bathroom. She's got that man who looked round our house coming back tomorrow, for another snoop. So I thought you'd help me.'

'Do what? What are you talking about, Alison?'

Alison rolled her eyes skywards. 'I daren't dye my hair at home (dumbos) because if I did I would get splashes (ner!) all over the carpets (which are green) and it would show and Mum would go mad because this man (she says) really, really, really likes our house, and he's the only one who's shown any interest for years, and his car was brand new, even if it was only a Ford, so he obviously has money, AND Dad said, "It's incredible that people can be so naive, but he didn't ask a word about the neighbours," so I'm dyeing it here.'

'But that's awful!' Caddy cried. 'Does your mother think she's actually found someone who wants to buy your house?'

'Why not?' demanded Alison, bristling. 'Why shouldn't he? There's nothing wrong with our house.'

'But then would you move?'

'No,' said Alison sarcastically. 'Obviously we'd live upstairs and he'd live downstairs! Dur! Of course we'd move. What's the matter with you, all of a sudden? We've been talking about moving for years.'

That was true. Alison's family's mythical, unlikely move to the place she could never remember the name of, had been common knowledge for years. Nobody believed in it, that was why they were surprised, any more than they believed any of the threats adults dangled over their lives. ('One day you'll wish you'd read those instructions properly!' 'Left your eyebrows alone!' 'Said, no!' 'Said, yes!' 'Stayed out of it!' 'Joined in!' 'One day you'll know what it's like to be always trekking up to school, making excuses for your daughter!' 'One day you'll look at a photograph and say, "Why did you ever let me go out looking like that?"' 'One day, you'll be paying the bills!' 'One day, when this house sells, we'll be out of here!')

Even Alison had not really believed that a house (no matter how neat) that was entirely green, as hers was, inside and out, walls, furnishings, carpets, kitchen and bathroom, would ever be wanted by anyone other than her green-loving parents. She herself did not like green. She preferred pink.

'But you can't just let them sell your house!' protested Caddy. 'You can't move, Alison! Aren't you going to do anything about it?'

'What sort of thing?'

'Put him off somehow! This man who's coming back again. Tell him something awful about it! Tell him . . . tell him it's haunted!'

'Mum and Dad always say nothing sells faster than a haunted house,' remarked Alison.

'Well then, say the roof leaks! Could you make a damp patch? Get into the attic and pour water through the ceiling!'

'They'd kill me,' said Alison.

'Well, do something with the electricity! Fuse all the lights! Leave something about that makes an awful smell! Block the loo with loo roll like they do at school! Get it overflowing! Could you fake a rat hole? *Don't you care?*'

'Whether I care or not, I can't do anything about it,' said Alison, shrugging. 'If he buys it, he buys it, but he probably won't. Either way, I can't change it.'

There was a sort of fatalism about Alison that words could not change. Arguing never worked with her. If anything, it made her more determined not to budge. Caddy gave up protesting, and picked up the box on the hay dressing table. '*No recreational colours!*' she remarked, quoting from the school prospectus.

'Or what?' asked Alison, mockingly. 'Like, what are they going to do? Cut my head off? I don't think so.'

'They could suspend you,' said Ruby.

'Well that would be fantastic!'

'But why,' asked Caddy, 'do you want pink hair?'

Alison said that she needed pink hair because she could not stand one more day of the hideous combination of black and purple school uniform and pale brown hair. 'Black and purple and *brown*,' she said. 'Think about it!'

They thought, and pointed out that half the school, at least, endured the same horrible fate. That Beth's hair was browner than Alison's and that even Caddy's gold and Ruby's red were really shades of brown.

'You squeeze this tube of stuff into this dispenser thing,' said Alison, utterly ignoring them as usual. 'Rub it in and leave it for at least half an hour.'

'It says you need gloves,' said Ruby, reading the instructions.

'I know. I've got some in my bag. And a towel. Help me put it on then! I don't want to miss bits.'

'You have to shake it up first,' said Ruby, still reading. 'With the top on! Oh well, it's only a drip! Let me do it!'

'Take your top off and put your towel round you,' suggested Beth. 'Gloves . . . you forgot the gloves!'

It was harder than it sounded. Random splashes appeared on everyone. The smell was so awful that Treacle took himself away to the far side of the field, and Beth's Norman diet could not cope with it. She lay on a hay bale, faint and giddy, while Caddy took Treacle's shampooing bucket to the house for hot water. Beth's mother was there, and Juliet too, eating green apple peelings and doing the splits.

'Is it true,' demanded Juliet, looking up from the floor, 'what Indigo and Saffron are saying at school? About the baby?'

'What about the baby?' asked Caddy.

'Something about how if anything awful happens to it . . .'

'Juliet!' warned her mother ominously.

'. . . if it does, about burying it in your garden . . .'

'Of course that's not true!' Caddy exclaimed indignantly, 'Indy and Saffron said that? I don't believe it!'

'I didn't say they said *exactly* that,' said Juliet warily.

'I'm sure they didn't!' said her mother. 'And don't ever let me hear you repeating such a thing again! How is the baby, Caddy?'

'I think it's all right,' said Caddy, uncertainly. 'The same as it was. We haven't been to see it because Saffy and Indigo got awful colds and they're still all sniffly, and I've caught it too, a bit.'

'There's all sorts going round,' agreed Juliet's mother. 'You can't be too careful.'

'Saffron and Indigo said the baby was all purple because it was too young,' continued Juliet, hooking another curl of apple peel, 'and they were going to dig—'

Juliet's mother reached down under the table and slapped Juliet with her spoon.

'There was a baby bird,' said Caddy, crimson-faced. 'A baby bird that we buried in the garden. You must have heard them talking about that.'

'Baby, they said,' repeated Juliet stubbornly, crawling out of reach of her mother's spoon. 'Nothing about birds. Is that pastry left over? Do you mind if I . . . ?'

Just in time, Juliet's mother rescued her pastry. Juliet stuck her thieving fingers in the sugar jar instead, sucked them and pushed them back, and was whacked on her bottom with the rolling pin.

'That's twice you've hit me,' said Juliet smugly. 'What if I ring Childline? Then you'll be sorry.'

'I dare say I will, but it's a very good idea,' replied her mother. 'Go on, off you pop! You haven't had a proper long chat with them for days!'

Juliet flounced out, flounced in again for a handful of raisins, and knocked the sugar off the table.

'Out!' roared her mother, so loudly Caddy jumped. 'Go on, out! Sometimes, Juliet, you are an absolute pest!'

'You should criticise the behaviour not the child,' Juliet told her primly as she left the room. 'We learned it at school in PSE. And they definitely said baby. Definitely.'

'I'm sorry, Caddy,' said Juliet's mother apologetically. 'I'm afraid she's showing off. Now, that bucket is very full! Shall I get the door for you? Has Beth got Treacle's shampoo with her there?'

'It isn't for—' began Caddy, crimson again.

'Wait till you dunk his tail,' said Juliet, reappearing. 'It's disgusting! He lifts it up and he does big . . .'

That was all Caddy heard before the door closed behind her. She heaved up the bucket and ran, and two minutes later was engrossed in the astonishing business of washing sugar pink bubbles from Alison's hair. And after that there seemed to be a tremendous amount of pink clearing up.

'Do you mind if I don't help?' asked Alison. 'Only there isn't a proper mirror here . . .'

Alison vanished.

'I'd better go as well,' said Ruby. 'They worry if I'm late.'

'Mum says "supper",' Juliet told Beth, appearing out of the twilight. 'She's in a mood, I don't know why, but you'd better come quick.'

'Is everybody going?' asked Caddy, in dismay. 'You

can't! We haven't worked out what to do about that man coming to Alison's house! It'll have to be us! She'll never do anything herself! I've had a sort of idea, but it might be too hard. Ruby! Beth! Can't you stay and talk?'

But Ruby was already leaving, with Beth and Juliet after her. 'Baked potatoes,' Juliet was saying. 'Ham salad. Apple pie. I helped make it. Hurry up!'

'Make sure the gate is shut.' Beth's voice came floating back to Caddy.

'Oh but . . .'

It was no good. They were gone.

It's nearly dark, realised Caddy, as she turned back to check the gate. The grass in the lane was damp with dew. In the streets the lights in the house windows shone yellow and homely. What a long day it had been, thought Caddy, trudging home. Pink everywhere, and Beth's mother's kindness. Juliet's awful conversation. Lost Property, where was he now? And what about their own fragile baby that they hadn't seen for days? Plus the worry about Alison's house . . .

Here it was now, with its For Sale board bumping in the wind. As Caddy passed she glimpsed the unusual sight of someone vacuuming a ceiling. Getting ready for tomorrow, she guessed. There was no sign of Alison, and her bedroom curtains were closed.

I've thought of something, Caddy told herself, thinking of the viewer expected at Alison's in the morning. And perhaps it will be better if I manage on my own.

'What have you done to your hands?' Saffron and Indigo and Bill demanded, as soon as she pushed open the door of home. 'What? What?'

'AlisonRubyanBethanme,' said Caddy (to Saffron's complete enchantment) 'dyed Alison's hair today.'

'*That* colour?'

'No. Much brighter.'

That night Alison was grounded. Utterly and completely. World without end. No hope of freedom ever again.

But not before Dingbat had seen the complete glory of her long, radiant, glimmering, fuchsia-coloured hair.

Chapter 17
Bill on the Doorstep

A windy autumn night and a damp drizzling dawn. Nine o'clock in the morning, and nobody at the Casson house dressed. Saffron and Indigo in their pyjamas eating toast and watching TV. Bill in his beautiful blue dressing gown making wonderful coffee from freshly roasted beans. Caddy safe in bed, wondering what would happen next.

So far not a soul had glanced out of a window.

Just as well: the view was frightful. Newspaper blown all over the street. Sheets of it burrowing under hedges, and wrapped round fences and railings. Soggy grey lumps on the road, squashed into pulp by the traffic. Nothing compared to the sight of the Casson garden though, from which the litter clearly originated. Not just newspaper either, but old clothes, abandoned toys, and even a couple of tarnished, tatty Christmas trees. Every now and then, and horribly prominent, an empty green bottle or two.

It looked for all the world as if someone had thrown the contents of the attic out of the attic window, let loose half a dozen newspapers in a gale, got drunk among the wreckage and crawled back inside to bed.

Alison's mother, raving on the Casson doorstep, eyes bright with fear, dredged up a word from the backmost corners of her memory and hurled it at Bill.

'Slummocky!' she screeched.

'Good Lord in Heaven!' exclaimed Bill, cradling his coffee cup. 'What on earth has happened? I shall take this very seriously. Thank you so much for your concern.'

'Slummocky!' she screeched again. 'Look at it! A disgrace!'

'It certainly is,' agreed Bill, picking up a sheet of newspaper between his fingertips. 'Yesterday's *Telegraph*! I hardly had a chance to look at it.'

'Bottles!' she continued, still raving! 'Mucky old clothes! Do something! I've someone coming, any moment . . .'

At that point disaster in the form of a brand new silver Ford pulled up at the kerb.

'Oh, I could howl!' moaned Alison's mother, and howl she did while the owner of the car climbed out, picked up *The London Review of Books* trampled at his feet, and said, 'Ah.'

So Bill (still in his Jaeger dressing gown, still cradling his fragrant coffee) stepped forward, introduced himself, shook hands, observed that a violent, but highly localised newsprint whirlwind (of rather distinctive quality) appeared to have hit the neighbourhood, and reassured his new silver Ford-driving admirer of the unique nature of the event. By the time Alison's mother had recovered enough to join them, they were discussing French red wines, the dismal nature of regional art galleries and the train service to London as if they had known each other for years.

'You will miss your neighbours,' commented the silver Ford man as he followed Alison's mother to her house, and Alison's mother knew then that as far as the house sale went it was a done deal.

'You have no idea,' she said, smiling bravely, and led him up to Alison's room which would make a rather nice study, being, as Alison's mother explained, exceptionally quiet and catching the morning sun. It caught a beam just as she spoke, proving all she said was true.

'A lovely tranquil room,' agreed her listener, and so it was, the lovely tranquility having been achieved earlier that morning by the ruthless exclusion of pink-headed teenagers. Alison had been whisked off at dawn ('We don't want him to think we're hippies') for a Saturday drive with a bag on her head. ('I suppose you would like me to put a bag on my head!' she had snarled at her father, and he, equally unpleasantly, had snapped back, 'Yes I would!' and regretted it later when the police pulled him up.) (But by then, as Alison's mother said jubilantly, nothing mattered.)

Meanwhile, at the Casson house, Bill was making an announcement.

'I am offering,' he said, laying a roll of bin bags down on the table, 'five pounds for the first one filled, and three pounds each for all subsequent offerings. Nobody touch the glass, I'll deal with that. Caddy, you can take the road, but stay on the pavement and watch out for traffic. You have fifteen minutes to get some clothes on, get outside and make your fortunes. After that time no further payments will be made.'

Then he looked at Caddy and added, 'There will be no recriminations.'

That was typical of Bill. No one was more at home than he in a disgraceful situation. Nor did he apportion blame, sinner that he was. Never, Caddy knew, would he question her involvement. And he was enjoying himself. He enjoyed being irresistible. He liked spending money. He hadn't even minded being screeched at from the doorstep. He smiled when he caught Caddy gazing at him, dropped one eyelid and murmured conspiratorially, 'I'd say we carried that off!'

The litter was all gone long before the silver Ford was driven away. Bill and its owner exchanged glances as it left. They smiled at each other in mutual comradeship and congratulation, Bill raising his coffee cup, the silver Ford owner raising his eyebrows, each saluting the other's ability to spend money rapidly and well.

Alison's mother never told anyone what she said to Bill on the doorstep that morning, and she never, ever used the word again.

Alison remained invisible.

Chapter 18
Starry Eggs and Moon Tomatoes

For Caddy, the weekend was redeemed from complete disaster by the arrival of her mother on Sunday afternoon. Owing to Bill's belief that everyone should stick to doing what they did best this happened very rarely, Bill's best not being the ability to spend time alone in special care baby units without going mad. Still, every now and then he abandoned his principles and did it, and then Eve would rush home to see how they were managing without her.

'Mummy, Mummy, Mummy!' they shrieked, engulfing her.

'Darlings, darlings, darlings,' she cried, gathering them in.

For the first hour it seemed that there were not words enough to explain to her all the things they had to say. Saffy and Indigo, especially, had to supplement them with action, dragging their mother by her arms to peer into the fridge, inspect the graveyard, gasp at Lego constructions, and examine scraped knees, crumpled school work, Old Panda washed within an inch of his life and now slowly recovering in the airing cupboard, the bags of rubbish piled by the back door, the faint pink still visible on Caddy's hands. It was a long time before they were exhausted enough to listen to their mother's news, and still longer before they were calm enough to look at the photos on her camera.

However, the photographs came out at last, and there was the same old hospital scene, same nest of tubes and wires, same purple occupant.

Only not the same.

'Is that the right one?' asked Indigo.

'Yes.'

'Is that thing a bandage?'

'It is, actually.'

'That huge thing?'

'We didn't tell you in case you worried, but she had a little operation, earlier in the week.'

Saffron and Indigo gave each other a look. A thoughtful look. *We must be more vigilant*, it said. *We should have found out about that.*

'A little operation?' asked Indigo suspiciously.

'Well, not huge.'

'On her side?'

'Well, no, that's where they . . . that's where they worked. On her heart, as a matter of fact.'

Caddy, who had been listening in shocked silence, gave a little sob of horror.

'Her *heart*?' repeated Indigo, and Saffy said, 'But isn't her heart *inside*?'

'Yes, yes it is.'

'So under that bandage is there a hole? And her heart?'

'Goodness no! Nothing like that! It's all beautifully closed up and she is doing wonderfully!'

'What did they do to her heart?' asked Caddy in a very small voice.

'Oh, Caddy!'

'Cut it?'

'No. Well yes. There was a part that was not working properly.'

'So did they mend it?'

'Yes! Yes! In a way. They took it out, and made a join. It's not uncommon. You'd be surprised. And now she is already much, much better! Look at the photos! See how she has changed!'

Except for the bandage, Caddy could see no change.

'She's breathing on her own now,' said Eve, 'isn't that wonderful?'

'Is it?' Caddy was not convinced. After all, even

her fledgling bird had breathed on its own.

'You wait till you see her! You could have done sooner, but it would have been such a risk, with those colds. Never mind, she'll be home before you know it.'

'Then we will have fireworks,' said Indigo, although less certainly than before.

'Oh yes! Rockets! How many rockets did you say?'

They shook their heads, they couldn't remember, although they knew it was a lot. Still, Eve's words were encouraging. The rockets had not been forgotten.

'Is she still the firework baby then?' asked Indigo, and Eve said yes, certainly, of course, what did you think and what shall I cook for supper before I go back to the hospital? Starry eggs with moon tomatoes?

That cheered even Caddy, because starry eggs with moon tomatoes were the thing Eve cooked best, and enjoyed cooking most, and as far as anyone in the family had ever been able to discover no other mother in the world had ever cooked them. 'No wonder,' said Eve. 'I invented them myself.'

'Daddy won't like them though,' remarked Saffron. 'He only likes healthy food.'

'Who says they're not healthy?' asked Eve. 'I'll make some for him as well. He can have a surprise.'

She said that, but in the end she did not make them.

It was Saffy, who with a star-shaped cutter, cut star-shaped holes in slices of brown bread. It was Indigo who broke eggs in a little jug, and stirred them until they were smooth and yellow. It was Caddy who fried the star-cut slices in olive oil until they began to brown, and then carefully, carefully, a little at a time, poured yellow egg into the stars, just enough to fill them, and after a breathless wait while the egg turned solid, flipped them gently over to brown on the other side. All Eve did was slice tomatoes into tomato half-moons and wash some lettuce leaves.

Star after star Saffron cut, egg after egg Indigo broke, slice after slice Caddy cooked, until they had the large blue platter full of yellow stars in golden skies, trimmed with tomato moons and lettuce leaf clouds, and all, as Saffron pointed out triumphantly, made out of the horrible health food Bill kept in the fridge.

At the moment of perfection Bill came home, stared in surprise at their stellar creation, managed not to exclaim, 'But you don't eat brown bread, or omelettes, or salad!' and said instead, 'Is this a miracle or just an illusion?'

It was an illusion, Caddy thought, an illusion like a bubble of sunlight, enclosing them, and holding them safe. All through supper it seemed to expand and grow warmer. All through supper Caddy was careful not to shatter it, and she could feel the others being careful too. They talked of gentle things, like the astonishing whiteness of Old Panda's newly washed face, and Indigo's recent haircut, begun by Saffron, interrupted by Bill, concluded by a hairdresser. ('I like it now,' said Indigo heroically, although he had been far from pleased at the time.) They talked most carefully of all of the firework baby, discussing possible names, not heart surgery. ('Everyone has a name,' said Saffron. 'Even if they're . . . Anyway. It's a pity she's not a dog 'cos we could call her Rocket. That would be a good firework name.'

They talked of their wonderful supper.

'Starry eggs!' said their father, as they ate together. 'Starry eggs are wonderful! How is it that we have never had them before?'

'We often do,' said Caddy.

'When you go back to London we have them,' said Saffron.

'To cheer us up,' explained Indigo.

'What!' exclaimed Bill, immensely pleased, and feeling fonder of his children than he had for days. 'Do you need cheering up when I go to London? I never knew that! Do you need cheering up when I go to other places too?'

They shook their heads.

'Just London?'

They nodded.

'But what's the difference?'

'You have to come back from other places,' explained Indigo. 'You can't stay there.'

'You've got a bed in London,' said Saffron. 'Haven't you?

Her father admitted that this was true.

'So,' said Saffron, 'you don't have to come back.'

Her father looked at her in astonishment. And then at Indigo, and then at Caddy and Eve. He looked at them as if to say, 'Did you ever hear anything so absurd?'

They looked back as if to reply, 'On the contrary. We never heard anything so reasonable.'

'But,' said Bill, clearly shaken to his heart, 'I always come back.'

The bubble of happiness strengthened and grew brighter. It held even after supper when Eve had to go.

'Tell the firework baby to get better,' Indigo commanded, hanging round her neck. 'Say "getbettergetbettergetbetter" like that.'

'Tell it about the rockets,' said Saffron.

'Yes, and tell it to hurry up.'

'Tell it about supper. Tell her I did the stars.'

'Tell it my bed smells funny,' said Indigo. 'And Saffy's bed smells very funny!' (Bill groaned, and ran upstairs.)

'Tell it about our graveyard,' said Saffron.

'Yes, tell it about our holes,' agreed Indigo. 'Tell it if it di—'

Saffron clamped two hands over Indigo's mouth, dragged him to the ground, and lay across his head. Bill came running down the stairs with an armload of sheets, fell over them both and said, 'Bedtime.'

'Tell it Daddy's a smelly pig,' said Saffron from the floor. 'And tell it Indigo bit me.'

'I didn't!' cried Indigo. 'Don't tell it that! I just closed my mouth!'

'On my arm,' said Saffron. 'Like this . . . ! OY! Daddy! Hey, put me down!'

'No, don't!' said Indigo. 'Take her away!'

Bill took them both away, one under each arm like bundles of laundry. Caddy and Eve were left alone together.

'You do look tired,' said Caddy, suddenly noticing the purple shadows under her mother's eyes.

'Only a little bit,' said Eve.

'When you come home I'll help you and help you,' promised Caddy.

'I know you will,' said her mother, hugging and hugging. 'Bye bye, darling Caddy. Don't worry

175

too much about anything.'

'Bye bye,' said Caddy and hugged and hugged her back.

Chapter 19
Caddy on the Doorstep

At just after seven on Monday morning Bill climbed the stairs, poked his head around the corner of Caddy and Saffron's room and said, 'Visitor to see you, Caddy. Hmmm.'

'What?' asked Caddy, still half asleep. 'Who? To see me?'

'To see me too?' asked Saffron brightly, emerging from underneath Old Panda and a collapsing pile of bears.

'Nope. Just Caddy. Paperboy, but he doesn't look up to the job. Rang the bell and asked to see you. Said it was urgent, so I told him to wait.'

'But I don't know any paperboys,' protested Caddy. 'We don't even have papers delivered! Anyway, I'm not dressed.'

'High time you were though,' said Bill, preparing to leave. 'I'll tell him to hop it then, shall I? I don't mind doing that.'

'No, no, I'll come,' said Caddy rolling out of bed and heading for the bathroom. 'Tell him to wait.'

Caddy pulled on scattered bits of uniform while searching her thoughts for possible reasons for her visitor. She had no idea, but when she arrived at the door she recognised the boy waiting there at once. He was a hanger-on of Dingbat's, a bony, giggling, fidgety individual. A sheepish sort of creature to find on a doorstep.

'Oh it's you,' said Caddy.

'Yeah,' said the sheepish one, staring vaguely down into a a huge fluorescent orange newsbag that he had dumped on the doorstep. 'I've come with a message. S'not good, Caddy.'

'What's not good?' asked Caddy, shivering a little. There was a chilly autumn breeze that morning. It was shivering weather.

'What Dingbat said to tell you.'

'Is Dingbat all right?' asked Caddy, truly alarmed, and at that moment she realised how very fond she was of Dingbat. And had been for so long. And even dimly that, all the time, sharing him had been a kind of way of keeping him. Which was necessary, because in a haphazard, Caddyish way there were times when she adored him . . .

'Dingbat's fine,' said the sheepish one. 'Dingbat's great! No worries there! Only, what he said to tell you was, he's gonna have to . . . well, it's done already. I'm afraid he said you're . . .'

The sheepish one was finding this surprisingly hard, which was not at all what he had expected. *'You go past Caddy's in the mornings, don't you?'* Dingbat had asked him the night before. *'Do me a favour and stop off and let her know it's over.'*
   'Like, dumped?'
   'Yeah, like dumped.'

'Dumped,' said the sheepish one to the shivering Caddy on the doorstep.
   'Dumped?'
   'Yeah.'
   The sheepish one now cheered up, the worst part of his message being delivered. 'So, now, if you like . . .' he continued much more confidently, 'since it's over with you and Ding, I thought, you and me . . . We could go out. That's why I said I didn't mind telling you. So I could get in quick to ask.'
   'I don't believe it,' said Caddy, dazed.
   'Believe it,' said the sheepish one, looking at his watch.

'But why?'

'Fancied you for ages!'

'NO! No. Why did Dingbat . . . ? Why has he . . . ?'

'Oh,' said the sheepish one. 'Ali. You know, Ali with the pink hair? She's why.'

'*Alison?*'

'You should have seen him when he met her on Friday night. When he saw that hair. "Ali, Ali, Ali!" he goes! He was nearly on his knees! So yesterday, he says to me, "Tell Caddy it's finished." And get her to tell the other two . . .'

'*Ruby and Beth?*'

'That's them.'

'I'm to tell Ruby and Beth?'

'He said it would be nicer, coming from you.'

'Nicer!'

'Well, I've not got time to do it,' said the sheepish one, picking up his bag. 'I'll be late as it is. I only said I'd tell you so I could ask about us.'

'It can't be true, it can't be true!' wailed Caddy. 'And don't say us like that! It sounds awful!'

'Awful!'

'Yes.'

'Forget it then,' said the sheepish one, highly offended. 'There's plenty of others'd be grateful. So forget it. Snooty cow!'

180

His last remark did Caddy good. She became Caddy incandescent, kicked the orange bag off the doorstep, and hurled shut the door.

'What on earth was that all about?' demanded Bill, shooting out from the kitchen.

'Only that I've been dumped,' said Caddy, and found herself in tears.

'My poor pet,' said her father, gathering her up. 'My poor, poor pet,' he said, stricken, not so much because she was dumped, as that she, his little Caddy, aged twelve, was in a position to be dumped. Aged twelve! he thought rocking her. What were young people coming to? He himself, he remembered, had been well past thirteen when he first broke a heart . . .

'He was nowhere near good enough for you,' he told Caddy, stroking her hair. 'What do you want with a twitching, miserable newspaper boy?

'It wasn't him. He just came to tell me.'

Caddy snuffled unhappily, and her father felt a pang of guilt, remembering dumpings long ago, when he too had sent a friend . . .

'Fancy not even telling me himself!'

'Perhaps,' suggested Bill, 'he thought it would be nicer . . .'

Caddy's snuffling became much deeper and wetter.

'Obviously not!' said her father, somewhat guiltily.

'Who was he anyway? What's he called?'

'Ding,' said Caddy, sniffing hugely. 'Dingbat.'

'Well, that's not even a real name!' exclaimed Bill, with sudden jubilance. 'Nobody's called Dingbat! Not in real life!' And he became very cheerful, as if not a real name meant not a real boy and no one worth crying over. (Certainly no one worth crying over brand new lambswool hand-wash-only jumpers.) 'Come on, Caddy!' he said bracingly. 'No more tears! That's enough! Love 'em and leave 'em, I say! It's always worked for me!'

Surprisingly, this revealing advice seemed to do Caddy good. She gave her eyes one last rub, and said she must go to school. And ten minutes, a slice of toast and a banana later, she was gone.

'That's my girl!' said Bill.

Chapter 20
Bravest of the Brave

The reason for Caddy's sudden decision to hurry to school was that in the depths of her father's jumper she had realised something. And what she had realised was that whether she liked it or not, she must warn Ruby and Beth.

It's not fair, she thought bitterly, but fair or not, it was true.

Ruby and Beth did not know they were dumped. As far as Caddy knew, they would be as hurt as she was. And if she did not get to them in time they would arrive at school thinking all things were well, and would probably discover the horrible truth in front of Alison and a hundred curious onlookers.

So what choice do I have? thought Caddy. None. None at all. It was outrageous, but the fact was, in the end, it would be nicer (as Dingbat said) coming from her.

So Caddy set out to meet her friends, and break the news of Dingbat's perfidy and Alison's treachery before they got to school. Half running, and half walking, past Alison's house (no wonder her curtains had been closed all weekend! No wonder she had not dared to glance out!). Past the Academy Head getting into her car. Past the sweet shop, in front of which Alison's pink hair had nearly brought Dingbat to his quivering knees. Past the yew trees from which the fledgling had fallen, and over the crossroads at the foot of the hill.

Then suddenly, there was Ruby. She was drifting along amongst the shoals of people hurrying towards school, red head down, completely engrossed in whatever she was reading.

'Ruby!' shouted Caddy, hurrying to catch up, and she called her name again as she ran.

'Ruby! Ruby!'

Still Ruby did not look up, and Caddy was not surprised. Ruby rarely heard the outside world when she was reading, especially on such a gusty, trafficked, busy autumn morning as this.

'Ruby!' called Caddy and the wind blew her voice away, and her hair into her mouth, and Ruby's curls into her eyes, and it blew the thing that Ruby was reading out of her hands. It whirled, in loose flying pages, into the road.

'Oh!' cried Ruby, leaping after it, and as she leaped several things happened at once. A lorry came speeding far too fast down the hill, a car braked, and the whole street full of walkers and students and drivers saw Ruby stumble and sprawl on the road.

Right in the path of the speeding lorry.

Everything Caddy was holding, jacket, bag, handful of dinner money, fell to the ground as she hurled herself after her friend.

Ruby was caught in a time warp. In one lifetime she had walked along a windy road. In another she lay bound to the ground in front of certain death, fear-stricken into immobility. In the long, long time in between she knew all she had lost. Decades of family history passed through her thoughts, and parallel with them, all the bright future of friendships and learning and discovery that might have been hers.

And then she saw Caddy, and knew what Caddy was going to do and, flat on her front, rigid with terror though she was, she screamed, 'Don't!'

Bad enough to die yourself. Unthinkable to take a friend with you.

'No!' shrieked Ruby. 'Don't!'

And then it was over.

Caddy caught hold of her friend by a wrist and her jacket, and just in time she pulled her from under the wheels of the lorry. Then, from those who had not hidden their eyes in horror, a great noise went up. It was as if the whole blustery autumn morning gasped with relief.

After that there was a great surge of movement as everyone within reach began racing towards Caddy and Ruby. Bystanders who had watched, or not watched, converged towards them. The driver of the lorry, who had managed to pull up several metres further down the road, came bellowing. Mrs Warbeck, the Head of the Academy, leaped from her car, grabbed both girls as if she owned them, and turned to face him.

'How dare you?' Caddy heard her demand. 'How dare you drive at such speed down such as street as this?'

The next thing anyone knew the driver had turned, sprinted back to his lorry, leaped into the cab and vanished, a moment captured by at least twenty people on mobile phone cameras.

The same number surrounded Caddy and Ruby, all wanting to touch or speak or simply stand and stare. This was horrible. Caddy and Ruby, dazed by all that had happened so quickly, backed away trembling until Mrs Warbeck came to their rescue.

Mrs Warbeck was excellent in situations like this. She pushed the girls behind her, clapped her hands until she had the crowd's attention, thanked them for their concern, and by the sheer power of expecting their co-operation, sent them on their way.

Ruby and Caddy gave great sighs of relief as time, under Mrs Warbeck's direction, once again moved forward. Walkers remembered their destinations. The traffic began to flow. Caddy collected her scattered belongings. Ruby rubbed her bumps and licked her grazes. The pages from the Academy prospectus fluttered to rest in the gutters. They were all that was left to show that anything had happened. That, and Mrs Warbeck, busy making calls on her own mobile phone.

'Ruby,' said Caddy. 'Are you OK?'

'I told you not to come,' said Ruby furiously, now shaking more than ever. 'Didn't you hear me? What if you'd got hit? What then?'

'Ruby!'

'What if you'd died?'

Never before had Caddy seen Ruby so angry.

'What else could I do?' she asked, stammering in her surprise. 'I was right behind you. I was looking for you. I'd been calling your name and trying to catch you up for ages! I had to tell you about Dingbat.'

'Dingbat!'

'Dingbat's finished with us.'

'So what does that matter?' demanded Ruby, still

flaming with shock and anger.

Caddy didn't know how to reply. Ruby, having passed from one life to another and back again in less than five minutes, seemed somehow in her journey to have left Dingbat behind.

'I don't know,' said Caddy at last. 'But I've got to find Beth. Will you be all right if I go?'

Ruby shrugged.

It was as if she had left Caddy behind too.

Caddy looked at her, puzzled, started away, came back, seized Ruby's hand and pulled her towards Mrs Warbeck, now finishing the last of her phone calls.

'This is Ruby,' she said. 'She wants to come to your school . . .' Caddy's eyes wandered to the scattered pages of the prospectus, still visible in the road. 'She wants and wants to come! But she's . . .'

'Caddy!' exclaimed Ruby pulling away.

'. . . scared. Talk to each other!' ordered Caddy and ran.

Mrs Warbeck had a voice that she used so rarely many of her students had never heard it. It was her disobey-me-at-your-peril voice, and she used it now.

'Come back at once!' commanded Mrs Warbeck, and when Caddy did not come back she turned to Ruby and asked (astonished), 'Who is she?'

Ruby could not answer at once because her shock

had turned to tears, and with the tears, her anger had vanished.

And so had her friend, who had given her back her life.

'She's Caddy,' Ruby told Mrs Warbeck at last. 'Cadmium Casson. Bravest of the brave.'

Chapter 21
Beth and Mars Bars

Juliet had a new preoccupation: Mars bars. Mars bars, Mars bars, Mars bars, thought Juliet, not quite all the time, but more or less. Mars bars in great quantity, such as she was never allowed.

Her mother bought her one. One! As a treat.

'One?' said Juliet, ungratefully. 'What good is one? Beth had about twenty!'

'Give it back if you don't want it,' said her mother cheerfully.

'How many did you buy Beth?'

'None. She's already had far too many.'

That cheered Juliet up a bit. She took her Mars bar and put it on her bedside table.

'Aren't you going to eat it?' asked her mother, astonished, but Juliet shook her head. She didn't want it to eat; she wanted it to own. She gloated over it in private and imagined a pocket full. How many wrappers had there been in that jacket pocket of Beth's? Not twenty, that had been an exaggeration. Ten? Probably less. Five or six? Five or six, Juliet thought, was about right.

'*Five or six!*' she told her single Mars bar incredulously. 'And I bet she had more, in other places!'

Juliet became a Mars bar detective, and she detected, with great cunning and stealth, all through her sister's pockets, and in the odd corners of her school bag and in the drawer of her desk. And in all these places she discovered Mars bar wrappers. Not hundreds, but more than ten. Maybe truly as many as twenty.

'I didn't even know she liked them that much,' said Juliet.

Beth did not like them at all. Mars bars made her sick.

The first time it happened was when she had eaten the three Mars bars on the way to school. That had been by accident.

The second was very privately, the following day, a morning when the Norman diet had failed Beth (or she had failed the Norman diet) and she had consumed peanut butter sandwich after peanut butter sandwich, ravenously, like a starving dog.

Regretted it.

Two Mars bars.

Gone.

Not pleasant. Horrible, in fact. But better than being full to bursting with bread and butter and peanuts.

After that it usually only took one. Sometimes not even that. Sometimes just the chocolatey, dark, slightly oily smell that came when the wrapper was torn open.

'I can't believe it,' said her mother, long afterwards, and looking back on the time herself, Beth also couldn't believe it.

But it was true.

On Monday morning, the same morning that Dingbat via the sheepish one dumped Caddy on her own doorstep, and Caddy via the path of a speeding lorry pushed Ruby into the arms of the Head of the Academy, Juliet came down from her bedroom in an unusually unselfish and kindly mood, and began to make breakfast. Large banana and raspberry jam sandwiches, dropped into a toasted sandwich bag and cooked in the toaster.

The sweet nutty smell of them was so appallingly delicious that Beth could not bear to stay in the house. She went to visit Treacle in his stable, and while she was there she ate a good deal of hay.

She did not come back until she judged that the

torment would be over, but she timed it completely wrong. When she returned Juliet was watching a jug of hot chocolate go round and round in the microwave. A large jug.

'I made enough for you as well,' said Juliet with pride. 'And I made you a sandwich! There on the table! I invented the recipe all myself. Go on, have it! They're lovely!'

There was nothing Beth could do but eat it. And afterwards there was nothing she could do but drink her hot chocolate.

'If we had marshmallows we could float them on the top,' said Juliet. 'Never mind, we've got squirty cream!'

'Oh Jools! No thank you!'

'Too late!' said Juliet cheerfully. 'Beth?'

'Mmmm?' asked Beth, digging through cream so thick she needed a spoon.

'What happened to your boots?'

'What?' asked Beth, startled.

'Your cowboy boots that you wouldn't let me wear.'

'Oh, them. They're somewhere around.'

'Could I borrow them for drama? Because we're all making plays in groups, and my group is doing *Puss in Boots*. I chose it. And I'm Puss. I arranged the whole thing because of your boots. So can I? Can I? Can I?'

'They'd be much too big.'

'That wouldn't matter because I'm a cat. All boots are too big for a cat! So is it all right?'

Beth groaned, partly because of the hot chocolate and toasted sandwich resting so uneasily on her Norman conscience, partly because of Juliet's phenomenal persistence.

She groaned, but gave in.

'All right. I don't care. They're put away somewhere.'

'I'll find them!'

Juliet was gone, prudently vanishing before her sister could change her mind. Beth was left sitting at the crumby breakfast table, and worrying that once again she had failed to meet the standards of the Norman diet. Worse still, she was penniless, her last pocket money having been withheld by her mother until she heard what it was to be spent on. 'Since you've had more than enough Mars bars!' her mother had said.

Hot chocolate with cream. Banana. Butter. Jam. Toast.

A large amount of hot chocolate, banana, butter, jam and toast.

I must get hold of a Mars bar, thought Beth in desperation and she called upstairs, 'Jools!'

'What?'

'Have you got any money?'

'Not real money,' said Juliet, who kept a china pig stuffed with toy money, tokens, Monopoly notes and foreign coins, none of which the sweet shop would ever accept. 'Everyone in our play group wanted to be Puss.'

'So?'

'So I had to bribe them,' said Juliet, in a surprised isn't-that-what-everyone-does? voice. 'I can't find your boots anywhere.'

Her voice was muffled, as if she couldn't breathe easily. It came from Beth's bedroom, and when Beth went up to investigate, she found her there. The only parts of Juliet that were visible were her feet sticking out from under the bed. The entire room looked ransacked (which was not surprising, because it had been).

Juliet's own bedroom, Beth noticed through the open door, was quite the opposite. Everything immaculately neat as always. All Juliet's possessions lined up in straight lines.

All of them clearly visible.

Including the most recent.

The temptation was too much for Beth.

She stole the Mars bar.

'I'll go to the stable and look for the boots there!' she called to the sticking out feet, and ran.

All the way up the hill Caddy had searched for Beth, hurrying against the flow of school-goers, right back to the turn-off to Beth's house, along the lane, up to the kitchen door (swinging open but nobody in) and finally to Treacle's stable, from which came the sound of outraged exclamations.

'You stole my Mars bar! Stole it! Stole it! Stole it and gobbled it and NOW YOU'VE SICKED IT UP!'

And there was Beth, drooping on a hay bale beside a very nasty puddle, and Juliet, absolutely dancing with rage in the doorway.

'Look!' she shrieked, when Caddy arrived. 'Look what she's done! *THAT WAS MY MARS BAR!*' And she grabbed Caddy and hauled her in to inspect the actual evidence, now all mixed up with toast and hay and looking absolutely frightful.

'SHE STOLE IT!' roared Juliet, nearly falling over with her rage.

Caddy sat down and put an arm round Beth and said, 'Don't, Juliet, she's not very well.'

Beth sobbed. Retched, and sobbed again.

'WHAT A WASTE!' cried Juliet, as more Mars bar appeared. 'WHAT A PIG! WHAT A WASTE! WAIT 'TIL I TELL MUM!'

'Juliet, stop it!' said Caddy. 'Beth can't help it. She's

poorly. It must be a tummy bug. Saffy and Indigo said there was one at their school last week. Anyone can catch them. We stayed away from the hospital in case the baby caught it.'

Caddy's heart sank as she spoke. She wouldn't be able to go again now, not after being with Beth.

Beth understood what she was thinking. 'It's not a bug,' she said.

'No it's not!' agreed Juliet, still raging. 'It's pigness and stealingness!'

'Juliet!' begged Caddy, dropping straw on the awful patch to put it out of sight. 'Stop it! Don't be unkind! No one's sick on purpose . . .'

Beth's sobbing grew worse.

'It's Mars bars!' said Juliet. 'That's what it is! She eats them all the time. Hundreds of them! Thousands of them! No wonder she's sick!'

'I have to,' sobbed Beth.

'*What?*'

'I have to, I have to, I have to,' said Beth, while Juliet and Caddy stared. 'I hate it, but I have to!'

'But Beth, of course you don't . . .' began Caddy, and Beth said, 'Don't you understand *anything*? Mars bars make me sick.'

Juliet and Caddy stared.

'So when I eat too much . . .'

197

'You don't eat too much,' said Juliet, with scorn. 'You hardly eat a thing . . .'

Beth clutched her stomach.

'. . . except Mars bars!' said Juliet.

'I eat too much and I can't stop growing,' wailed Beth.

It became so quiet that they could hear Treacle's hoof steps, swishing through the long grass towards the stable door. He had gone away at the beginning of the shouting, but now he came plodding back and nudged Beth's drooping shoulders.

Caddy's face was completely puzzled. Juliet was the first to speak. She said, 'But you can't stop growing! You have to!'

'I don't.'

'Yes you do,' agreed Caddy. 'We all do. You, me, Ruby, Alison. Juliet. All of us.'

Beth groped past her and went to loop her arms round Treacle. She said, 'Treacle, Treacle.'

'Treacle?' asked Caddy. 'Is that why? Treacle?'

'Of course it is!' snapped Beth, and Caddy became silent again.

Juliet was beginning to understand at last. After all, more than anyone in the world, she was aware of her sister's growing. She always had been. It was part of her life.

'You grow out of things,' she said. 'And I grow into them. And then I have them. Mostly.'

'You're lucky,' said Beth.

'Lucky?' Juliet thought about that before she agreed. 'I mostly don't mind.'

Beth raised her head and looked at her in astonishment. It had never occurred to her that Juliet might mind.

'Well, I do mind the school jumpers,' admitted Juliet. 'Because they've always gone bobbly. They never look new. And when I had your old scooter it took ages to peel all the pony stickers off. Same with your desk when you got a new one for big school.'

'Oh.'

'And I mind very much,' continued Juliet (enjoying this good grumble), 'when teachers at school say "Oh you must be Beth's sister!" and say how nice you were and everything, compared.'

'Compared to what?'

'Compared to me.'

'They don't say that!'

'They think it though,' said Juliet. 'I've seen them.'

'When?'

'Lots of times! When I kept that money I found in the cloakroom. When I slapped yucky Josh when he tried to kiss me! When I posted my birthday sweets

199

down the playground drain so I didn't have to share them. That Christmas when I was Mary . . .'

'That was terrible,' said Beth. 'It wasn't funny. It was just awful.'

'I didn't mean for everyone to be so mad,' said Juliet. 'I only said . . . because it was a girl doll. And Jesus was a boy . . . Anyway, it just proves I'm not as nice as you. And I'm not like you. And I can't do the things you do.'

Juliet paused. And looked at Treacle.

Caddy looked at him too. And at Beth's sad, defiant face, and her long legs, and her hungry eyes.

'It won't work,' she said.

'What won't?'

'Not eating, and being sick. Trying to be Norman-sized! That's what you're doing, isn't it? I remember you talking about it! I thought it was a joke!'

'Well, you were wrong.'

'You'll have to think of something else, Beth. You could keep Treacle like a sort of pet, I suppose . . .'

'Very expensive, just for a pet,' said Juliet.

'What do you know about it?' demanded Caddy.

'Only what Mum and Dad say. When Beth's not there.'

'I don't believe it,' said Beth, but that wasn't true. She did believe it.

'It wouldn't be keeping him just for a pet if you would ride him, Juliet,' she cried. 'Oh Jools! Why won't you!'

Beth was crying again, but Juliet was shaking her head. Shaking it and shaking it, and backing away to the door as if somebody was about to make her ride Treacle right then.

'I won't,' she said. 'I can't. You can't make me. Not if you eat a million Mars bars and are sick a million times. You should let Treacle go back to the riding stable, that's what you should do! And stop wasting all the money! I'm going!' said Juliet, and went.

For a very long time neither Beth nor Caddy spoke. Caddy thought, school. They were beyond late, it must be nearly lunchtime. She thought Ruby. Alison. Dingbat. She thought of the firework baby, and that it couldn't catch Mars bar sickness, and that that was one good thing. She thought about Juliet's last words, and about Treacle and Beth. She remembered Treacle running to the fence in the hope of meeting ponies. He would probably be happy, back at the riding stables.

'Juliet's right,' said Caddy.

Beth shook her head.

So for the second time that day, Caddy was brave. Braver than the first time, because after all it is not very brave to drag your friend away from a speeding lorry if the alternative is worse: friend jam, all over the road. Instead Caddy was brave in a cold, knowing-the-consequences way. She said what nobody had so far dared to say.

'You're already much too big for Treacle, Beth. Already. Now.'

Then Beth said what Caddy had known she would say. 'I thought you were my friend. I hate you. Go away. Get out of here. I hate you I hate you for ever.'

Shouted it, with her fists clenched, and her eyes blazing, and her face white, and in the middle of her shouting Juliet appeared, and with her someone else.

'I telephoned Mum,' said Juliet, 'and she's here.'

Chapter 22
Pink Hair at School

Of all the girls, Alison was the only one to make it to school that Monday. Alison, and her world-stopping hair. Deep, deep fuchsia pink, shading to a luminous rose at the ends. Dingbat was not the only boy whose heart missed beats when he saw it. Alison stalked to school through a crowd that parted and sighed, 'Ahhh'.

Straight to the headmaster's office went Alison. 'To save them bothering to send me here,' she explained to him.

'I see.'

'Nobody in this school listens to anything I say.'

'I'm listening.'

'I don't mind being suspended.'

'No. I know that.'

'This pink. It looks pink, doesn't it?'

'It does.'

'It isn't. It's not real. It's an illusion. It's reflected.

The actual colour is the opposite. It's about light. It's everything not pink. Am I right?'

'You are right,' said the Head, and paused. 'Now, this student Alison. This don't-care, rebellious Alison. It's not real either, is it? It's an illusion. It's reflected. The actual Alison is the opposite. Am I right?'

Alison stared, shattered with horror at being so completely understood, and she thought with thankfulness of Tasmania, where no one had learned to read her mind.

'Anyway, I'm leaving,' she told the Head.

'If that is true, it's a great pity,' he said calmly. 'Our loss completely. Nevertheless, at this moment you are here. And your hair (which looks wonderful). So what am I to do? Suspend you? You wouldn't care. Chop your head off? Ridiculous!'

'What then?'

'Well, I'll ask you to think about it. Not in a rush, over the next few days.'

'Is that all?'

'And tie it back for science.'

'OK.'

'And try not to start a fashion.'

'Me?'

'Thank you, Alison.'

★ ★ ★

Dingbat caught up with her at lunchtime, following her out of the dining hall.

'Ali, Ali, Ali,' he called, mowing down Year 7s in his hurry to get to her. 'Ali, I love it! I need to talk to you, Ali. I need to tell you it's finished with Caddy and me!'

'*What?*'

'I finished it. It's over. Beth and Ruby too!'

'You finished it? Since when?'

'Since this morning.'

'But none of them are in school today.'

'Aren't they?'

'Didn't you notice?'

'I only noticed you,' said the mesmerised Dingbat, and Alison's heart lurched with sadness, because now it was too late. Her secret hope, that one day her three friends would grow tired of Dingbat and leave him to notice only her could never happen.

However, Dingbat musn't know.

'Is that why they're not here today? Caddy and Ruby and Beth? Because you dumped them?'

'I didn't dump them *personally*,' said Dingbat virtuously. 'I got a mate . . .'

'You got a mate?' repeated Alison, fell out of love in one blissful releasing moment, and turned her thoughts entirely to revenge.

'Well, it's nicer, isn't it, if you send a mate? Less, you

know . . . stressy. Anyway, you and me, Ali! How about it?'

She was just the right height for him to rest his chin in the pink hair. 'Mmm?' he said, resting it. 'OK? You and me? And listen to this idea I had, after I saw you the other night.'

'I'm listening,' said Alison.

'I do my hair a colour too! Pink even! Yes? What do you say? Because I think you have really great style, Ali! Special! Just like me!'

Alison stepped back to look at him. Dusty gold unravelling hair. Unrepentant green eyes. That smile.

'Would you really do that, Ding?' she asked, reaching out to hold his hand, smiling with pleasure at the lethal nature of her thoughts. 'Pink?'

'Tonight. Come and help me.'

'I can't. I'm grounded till the end of time.'

'Oh, Ali!'

'I know. Bye, Ding.'

Chapter 23
Saffron and Indigo on the Doorstep

Caddy wandered home from Beth's house so slowly that it was the middle of the afternoon before she arrived. She had a door key in her pocket, and she hoped the house would be empty.

It wasn't. As soon as she opened the door she knew that. She could hear her father upstairs. It sounded like he was moving furniture and not enjoying it. Something crashed, and Caddy heard a howl of pain, and then the telephone rang in the kitchen. Bill fell downstairs, grabbed it, caught sight of Caddy, stared till his eyes bulged, said, 'Yes, yes, thank you, she's here now,' and put down the receiver.

He said, 'Caddy.'

'Hello,' said Caddy. 'I'm back.'

School had rung. Ruby's grandparents had rung, all four of them. The police and the local paper had rung. Someone whose name Caddy's father could not catch had left a message on the answerphone on behalf of Dingbat. It said, '*Ding says if it doesn't work out with Alison he'll be right back.*' Eve had rung from the hospital saying everything was wonderful. Fingers crossed. Beth's mother had rung some time ago to say Caddy was on her way home. In between, said Bill, many people from London had rung including Bill's accountant who organised his income. ('When I'm allowed to earn anything,' said Bill.)

Everyone who had rung about Caddy had a different conflicting story: Caddy's friend had fallen in the road. Caddy, last seen, was hurrying to school. The driver of a lorry had been stopped several miles out of town. He'd been driving too fast, but he knew nothing about Caddy. Caddy was not hurt, but her friend had grazed knees and was rather shaken. The reason Caddy was not at school was that she was looking after another girl, who was sick. It was nothing infectious, and Caddy was on her way home.

'I've heard from half the English-speaking world,' said Caddy's father. 'So now let's hear from you.'

'I've had,' said Caddy, staggering to the sofa, 'I've had . . . I've had . . . I've had an *awful* day!'

Without being asked her father took off her grubby shoes, tucked her feet up on the sofa, fetched her a glass of milk and handed her Old Panda.

'Beth hates me,' said Caddy. 'And Ruby's going to the Academy. Dingbat's dumped me so he can have Alison instead but you already know about that. I expect I'll get in trouble about bunking off school but I didn't mean to. Beth was sick and I couldn't leave her. Her mum said she'd ring our class teacher to explain. Soon there won't be any stable den, or anyone to go there with. And I haven't had any lunch.'

Caddy did not get this whole statement out uninterrupted. Twice the phone rang and had to be answered. During one of the calls her father spoke very charmingly to someone repeating, several times, "I've never missed a deadline yet.' The next time he was more his usual self saying, 'I'm sorry. I'm sorry. I haven't time now. Perhaps you could tell me later. I may not be able to do that this evening. It'll be over very shortly, and then we'll all be able to move forward again . . . Don't set your hopes too high, darling.' It was only right at the end, when he came to the darling, that Caddy realised he had been talking to Eve.

At last he turned back to Caddy again, and Caddy began to tell him more things. About Mars bars and hay and how Ruby, when reading, never really heard a word that anybody said. However, long before Bill had understood anything at all, Saffron and Indigo came bursting in from school, absolutely jubilant because after-school club had been cancelled.

'Cancelled, cancelled!' sang Saffron, flinging around cushions. 'Why've you got Old Panda, Caddy?'

'I haven't had any lunch,' said Caddy pathetically, and fell asleep at that moment, still holding her glass of milk.

'Look at Caddy!' marvelled Indigo, and Bill said, 'Don't wake her. Let her sleep a little while. She's had an awful day!'

Caddy slept through more phone calls. Through supper of eggs and toast and apple pie from a box. ('At last Daddy's learning to cook,' remarked Saffron.) She slept through her father beckoning, 'Come and look at this, you two.' She slept through Saffron and Indigo's squeals of astonishment and promises of silence. She slept while they dug in the garden and her father (with the phone switched off because Caddy was safe home at last) worked upstairs, undisturbable except in the direst of emergencies because this was a day when he'd had a hundred things to do, and not one of them was done.

It wasn't entirely peaceful sleep, however. Every now and then a lorry bore down on her. Someone screamed: 'I hate you!' Every now and then the baby at the hospital went cold and still.

Sometimes she surfaced enough to catch words:

'Did you hear Mummy's message? Do you think she was crying?'

'Is it something to do the baby?'

'Saffy, LOOK what I found! LOOK!'

'Don't tell Caddy. She's had enough today.'

'Is it a secret?'

'It is till tomorrow.'

'It's the best hole we've ever dug.'

'It has to be!'

In between Caddy slept, a restless, worried sleep. She dozed until the early evening and then woke to hear more voices.

Saffron and Indigo on the doorstep.

A reporter from the local paper had arrived.

Saffron and Indigo were hardly surprised. They had met reporters before. Both of their parents had been interviewed and photographed. *Local Artists Painting Duo Eve and Bill Casson* the headline (much to Bill's horror) had read.

The actual reporter on the doorstep that evening was a familiar face to Saffy and Indigo. She often visited school in the search for something to cover the acres of white paper she was expected to fill. Saffron had shot to fame at the opening of the new school wildlife pond, when she had volunteered to have her photograph taken. *Naturalist Saffy Walks on Water* it had been entitled

– and there was Saffy ankle deep and smiling, simultaneously demonstrating the efficiency of the submerged safety grill and pointing to a ripple where a frog might once have been. That was Saffron's moment of glory, and Indigo's had come not long afterwards, when a local writer had visited the newly decorated school library. She had asked for ideas for stories, and Indigo (all by himself, aged five) had stood up in front of everyone and delivered the plot for an entire new book. It was about dogs (Dalmatians, a hundred and one of them). 'There was one like it before,' Indigo had explained. 'And it was really good. You could do it again, with different dogs.'

The applause had been huge, and Indigo's smiling face had appeared under the confusing but attention-grabbing headline *Possibly the Next Harry Potter.*

Not surprisingly, after these happy experiences, Indigo and Saffron had taken a liking to public acclaim. They took to spending many happy hours 'playing newspapers' which meant interviewing each other on such pleasant subjects as biscuit preferences and clouds. So they were very pleased indeed to find a reporter smiling down at them when they opened the door, especially as she happened to be the same person who had written so admiringly of them in the past.

But it was a pity she asked to speak to their father.

'He's upstairs,' Saffron told her. 'And he absolutely must not be disturbed for any other reason except if the house is on fire.'

The reporter seemed rather disappointed about that.

'I wouldn't take long,' she said. 'Just a few words about your sister. I've heard the main story, several times. I would just like a little background.'

Saffron and Indigo looked at her unhelpfully. As far as they knew, Caddy had done nothing to deserve any sort of fame. They didn't know anything about main stories or backgrounds. They wanted to start playing newspapers.

'I telephoned,' the reporter told them, 'several times.'

'Lots of people do,' said Indigo nodding.

'It's about your sister, Caddy. I hear she has been very brave.'

Caddy, listening through the crack in the door, felt herself going cold with horror. The last thing she wanted, the absolutely last, was to talk to some stranger about the awfulness of her day. She retreated back to the sofa and the comfort of Old Panda. *Manage by yourselves!* she silently commanded Saffron and Indigo in her head.

Saffron and Indigo did. Life without their mother had taught them a great deal of independence. Managing by themselves was something they had learned how to do, over the last few weeks.

Recently school photographs had been taken. All three of them were lined up on the windowsill at that moment. They were clearly visible from the doorstep. Saffron noticed the reporter looking at them.

'I've a much nicer picture of Caddy than that,' she said, and ran upstairs. She came back a minute later, carrying the photograph taken on Ruby's birthday trip.

'There she is with all her friends,' she told the reporter proudly. 'That's Alison. That's Ruby. That's Beth. And that's Caddy. Do you know what they call Caddy? The bravest of the brave!'

The reporter looked for a long time at the photograph. She seemed to like it very much. She asked, 'Might I possibly be able to borrow this, please?'

'You'd have to give it back.'

The reporter said that would be no problem. 'Bravest of the brave,' she repeated, as she folded it carefully into her notebook. 'But where is she now? Is she here? Would she be able to talk to me?'

Saffron and Indigo looked at each other. Was Caddy able to talk? Yes. But in her sleep? No. Nor did they want to wake her to talk. They liked talking, and they preferred to keep reporters to themselves. They didn't want to share them.

Saffron and Indigo shook their heads, and said no, Caddy wouldn't be able to talk. However they themselves had nothing much to do, and could tell her anything she liked.

'We should need your father's permission first,' said the reporter.

That was easy. From the bottom of the stairs Saffron screeched 'Can we play newspapers with a newspaper lady?' and from his lair at the top Bill bellowed in reply, 'Do as you like but don't set the house on fire.'

'Can we make cups of tea?'

'No.'

'Biscuits?'

'You've just had supper! Oh, all right. One each. I'll be down in a few minutes.'

'Won't all that shouting have woken up your sister?' asked the reporter, still on the doorstep.

They said they didn't think so, and since she prudently refused to come in, they hospitably took a ginger biscuit out to her and pressed it into her hand.

'Tell me a little bit about your sister then,' she said. 'I hear she's very brave.'

That started them off at once, and they launched into descriptions of Caddy's bravery. They concentrated on spiders, the fat sort that looked squashy, and enormous sticky ones with loose legs.

'There's one lives in the cupboard under the sink,' said Saffron. 'It's horrible. As big as a hairbrush! But Caddy never lets anyone make it go away. She says under the sink is its home and it would be cruel to make it move. And if anyone wants anything out from there, Caddy puts in her hand and gets it.'

'That's brave,' Indigo told the newspaper lady and she shuddered and nodded.

'She was braver than that even with the frog,' continued Indigo excitedly. 'The frog that Daddy ran over with the lawn mower and cut off its legs and it didn't die and Daddy said it probably wouldn't feel a thing because it was a frog . . .'

'Bloody Daddy,' remarked Saffron.

'. . . Be quiet, Saffy, it's my turn talking! Because it was a frog, like I said. But Mummy couldn't look and Daddy said "Leave it, it's nature"—'

'Caddy said lawn mowers aren't nature,' interrupted Saffron.

'Shut *up*, Saffron! And Caddy said lawn mowers aren't nature and she picked it up and put it in a cereal bowl with cool water and killed it . . .'

'Killed it?' asked the reporter, sounding rather surprised.

'Yes, with one of Mummy's tablets melted in the water and the frog stopped twitching and went asleep and we buried it in the graveyard.'

'With a gravestone,' said Saffron. 'With writing on it. Come on. We'll show you.'

All the time this conversation was going on, Caddy had been on the sofa. She could hear the talking, but hardly any of the words that was said. She didn't want to. However, when she realised that the reporter was being taken to the garden she became suddenly curious. She crept across the little hall to peer out of the kitchen window. There were Saffron and Indigo, displaying the family graveyard.

'That's the frog,' she heard Indigo say, pointing to a gravestone made from a green plastic plate, 'and that's his name, written on it.'

'*Valium*,' read the reporter, spelling out the wobbly felt pen letters.

'After Mummy's tablet,' said Saffron.

The reporter gave her a very odd look, and then turned to another gravestone.

'*Lost Property.*'

'He had a good hole,' said Indigo. 'Square corners. It took ages. We've only just started doing square corner ones. Before that we just did round.'

'You dig the graves?'

'Me and Saffy,' said Indigo modestly.

'Then can I ask . . . ?'

What was she staring at, wondered Caddy. Which of the many Casson graves had brought that shocked note to her voice? She wasn't looking in the direction of the established graveyard now. Her face was turned towards the very end of the garden, which was so far uninhabited.

Faintly on the evening breeze, came a snatch of words from Indigo: '. . . that's for when the firework baby . . .'

Bill came downstairs.

Caddy heard his footsteps just in time to get back into living room, regain the sofa, and close her eyes. She heard the gentle opening of the door as he peeped in to check on her. Then his exclamation of surprise a moment later, when he found no Saffron and Indigo playing in the kitchen. Almost immediately after that, she nearly jumped out of her skin at his roar of indignation when he discovered an unknown reporter picking her way amongst the family gravestones, with never a word of permission. And then the reporter was escorted to her car and hurried off the premises, and Saffron and Indigo were sent upstairs for baths.

Caddy gave up pretending to sleep. She was sitting up with Old Panda when Bill came in again.

'Caddy, this girl you looked after today, I know her family were very grateful. Her grandparents telephoned and told me so. And something about a new school for her too, that seems to have pleased them a lot. And the police said you'd witnessed a speeding lorry, and I know your friend Beth was sick, and I quite understand about not leaving her . . .'

'Good.'

'But can you please explain why I just found Saffy and Indigo showing some woman from the local rag every hole they ever dug in the garden?'

'What did Saffy and Indigo say?'

'Some rubbish about you and spiders and her coming to their school.'

'Nothing about me picking up Ruby?'

'Nope, not a word.'

'I don't know then,' said Caddy wearily. 'I can't think. I feel all floppy and rubbishy.'

'You've had nothing to eat since you came in,' said her father. 'That's what's the matter with you.'

He cooked a special little omelette, brought it in on a tray, and stayed to keep her company while she ate it.

'Tell me about Mum and the baby,' said Caddy. 'You haven't been to see them today.'

'I have. I went this morning, after you lot had left. They were waiting for the doctor to come round when I came away.'

'Why did they need a doctor?'

'It's just routine, Caddy! Don't start panicking! It's a hospital! They do have doctors!'

'Are you sure?'

'The baby is fine,' her father told her. 'Eve's chosen a name at last, she says, but I'm not to tell you because she wants to do it herself.'

'It's been ages since we went to the hospital,' said Caddy a bit dismally.

'I know, but while you had colds and the good Lord in Heaven knows what it wasn't worth the risk. Not after that chest infection. And then surgery. Heart surgery's no joke.'

'I know,' said Caddy in a very small voice.

'We'll have them home before you know it!'

Promise, Caddy wanted to ask, but she didn't, and anyway, she knew he wouldn't. Not after the last home-before-you-know-it when the baby had been so ill.

'Bed for you, Caddy,' said Bill. 'You'll see them very soon.'

'When?'

'Tomorrow, all things being well.'

Chapter 24
Tomorrow, All Things Being Well.

Caddy went to bed, but she could not sleep. This time the genie had spun her world too hard, too fast, too recklessly. She had nearly lost track of how much she had lost. Deep in the night, the only one awake in the whole exhausted house, she counted.

No more Dingbat.

No more charmed circle. AlisonRubyanBethanme. No more. And what else, worst of all?

The baby.

'*Tomorrow*,' her father had said, '*all things being well*,' but in the darkest part of the night tomorrow seemed a world away to Caddy, and she had even less hope of all things being well.

Her father had told her, '*Don't worry*.' '*Fine*.' '*Coming home soon*.' That sounded all right, except he had also said, '*Heart surgery's no joke*.' Most telling of all, not knowing he was overheard, '*It'll be over very shortly and then we can all move forward.'* He had said to Eve, and Caddy had heard, *'Don't set your hopes too high, darling.'*

Also, thought Caddy, hugging her knees in the dark, there was something that Saffron knew and Indigo knew, and she did not. That was not surprising, and had happened before. Saffron and Indigo had told half their school about the night the baby stopped breathing and the alarms went off before Caddy heard a thing. She might never have known if it had not been for Juliet. 'The insight of the illiterate,' Caddy's father called their telepathic understanding of what the grown-ups tried hardest to hide. Saffron and Indigo knew when Bill was angry and Eve was miserable. They had private conversations with their father when they thought Caddy was asleep. *'Is it a secret?'* Caddy had overheard, and *'Do you think she was crying?'*

Caddy slipped out of bed and crossed the room to the sleeping Saffron.

'Saffy!'

Saffron burrowed deeper into her pillow.

'Saffy, wake up!'

'Whywhywhywhy?' moaned Saffron.

'I want to know about the baby. Have you heard anything new?'

Saffron rolled over in bed amongst her bears. With her soft tangled hair and her round sleepy eyes she looked like a baby angel tumbled into a zoo. She said reproachfully, 'I was bloody asleep, Caddy.'

'There's a secret about the baby and I want to know it,' said Caddy.

Saffron's mouth went very prim and tight and pouty. She let her eyelids droop. She slumped. 'We're not to tell you,' she said and went deliberately and unshakeably back to sleep.

Indigo was always so difficult to rouse that it was almost an act of cruelty to attempt it. However, Caddy was desperate. She joggled him, rolled him and froze him with no covers.

Indigo remained asleep. Caddy considered pouring water over him, but the last time anyone had tried that trick he had dreamily wet the bed. Instead, she tickled his feet, removed his pillow, and when that did no good, tipped him right out altogether. Indigo slept on amongst the toys and shoes on the floor, looking pathetic. Conscience-stricken, she heaved him back on to his mattress again, moving him in sections: head and shoulders, an arm and a leg. The bits left over.

He said, 'Sank you, Caddy,' with his eyes tight shut and held up his arms to be hugged. He said, 'In the morning I'll show you the hole. For.'

'For what?'

'For . . .' there was a long pause. 'For the . . .' an

immense pause. 'For the fire . . . work . . .'

The last words were so silent a murmur, from so far away, that they were no more than a breath. But they were enough.

'Thank you, Indy.'

Caddy dropped his quilt on top of him and tiptoed back to her room. In the miserable cold grey before dawn she dressed, and slipped downstairs, through the kitchen and into the garden.

Babies were not buried in gardens, Caddy knew. No baby would ever be buried in theirs. But Saffron and Indigo did not know that. Saffron and Indigo had more than once indicated that should the need arise, they would be ready to help. Caddy remembered very well the grave prepared for Lost Property, before he was dead they had known it would be needed and set to work. Juliet's remarks on the subject the night they dyed Alison's hair also came back to her, and the startled note in the reporter's voice only the evening before.

In the shadowy pre-dawn greyness the new hole looked shocking. A rectangle of darkness. Still. Quiet. But waiting.

Now there was a question to which Caddy had to know the answer. Was the baby dead?

Caddy pushed it to the back of her mind and ran.

It was a short drive to the hospital, only three or four miles. A long, long walk though, early in the morning.

The town woke up as Caddy scurried along its roads. Early dog walkers. Delivery vans. A street sweeper spinning its brushes in the marketplace. A flock of pigeons, silver and gold and pink and grey, rising from the library window ledges to circle and dip and spread for the day's gleaning on the streets below. Then the long road out of town with the wind suddenly much colder and a fierceness in the flow of the traffic. The hospital car park, three-quarters empty, an amazing sight to Caddy. Usually it was so overflowing that her father drove round and round in a state of increasing fury and ended up parking half on grass, half on yellow cross-hatched lines.

The huge glass doors were open. Deliveries were being carried in for the hospital shop in the foyer opposite the reception desk. Boxes and flowers and newspapers.

'Oy!' said the porter on the reception desk, catching sight of Caddy the moment she stepped through the doors. 'What are you doing here?'

Caddy looked at him nervously. She knew him fairly well by now. He always noticed them when they came in with Bill, and he always nodded. Two or three times he had actually emerged from behind his desk in time to catch Saffron before she bolted into the car park. Once he and Indigo had played a winking game, he with alternate eyes, Indigo, despite enormous efforts, with both at once, the porter very solemn, Indigo speechless with giggles.

One day, after Caddy had spent a long time dithering over the buckets of carnations in front of the hospital shop, he had even spoken. 'They're not allowed on the ward where she is, pet,' he had advised Caddy. 'Anyway, those prices are daylight robbery. Take your mum a paper. She'll like something to read.'

He had watched with approval when Caddy took his advice.

The porter always seemed to have a newspaper to hand. He was holding one now as he looked at Caddy, first off the pile for the shop, ink fragrant, and smooth as if it had been freshly ironed. A long headline and a colour photograph and the porter's eyebrows raised very high as he looked over it to Caddy.

'I've come to see my mum,' said Caddy, and when his eyebrows lifted even higher, 'I've got to.'

'Thought you'd got tired of coming here. Haven't seen any of you for more than a week.'

'We had colds and things. And everyone said better

not risk it.'

'Ah! And you are Cadmium Casson, is that right?'

'Yes.'

'You see, I know all about you!'

'Oh . . .'

'And as it happens, I know your mum is up and about because I just called through to where she is and sent the papers up to the ward.'

'Oh, did you . . . ?'

'Ten o'clock's visiting. You're more than three hours early.'

'I'm here now.'

'Yes you are. And you've got to see your mum. And since it's you, I'll forget the rules . . .'

'Oh, thank—'

'Ring through to the ward . . .'

'Oh no, you don't have to . . .'

'Put forward the clocks . . .'

Caddy's father often said that hospitals drove him crackers. He also often remarked that if he had to spend any length of time incarcerated behind a desk he would go crazy.

The hospital porter, as far as Caddy could tell, spent his days and nights incarcerated behind a desk in a hospital, and it seemed he had suffered the fate that her father had foretold for himself. His insanity took the form of speech:

'Since it's you I will roll out the red carpet that we keep for heroes . . .'

Crackers, thought Caddy, jiggling from leg to leg with impatience.

"Stand still and wait a minute longer . . . Scatter rose petals . . .'

He really was insane. Bonkers, nuts, both crazy and crackers. And terribly slow. He talked between pauses, first addressing Caddy, and then murmuring inaudibly into the phone he had just picked up.

'. . . and order a band! Off you go, pet! Here's someone coming to look after you.'

It was the nurse that Caddy had met on her very first visit; the one who was so careful about clean hands. She was just as careful now, in fact more so than ever: after one glance at Caddy's feet she produced overshoes for her to wear as well. Still, she was smiling and friendly. She led Caddy, not to the place for special care babies, but along to a perfectly ordinary glass-windowed corridor, with wards along one side and offices on the other.

Perhaps the hospital was not accustomed to early morning changes of routine. From all the doorways along the corridor heads popped out to look at Caddy as she passed.

One of them was Eve, clutching a newspaper. She let it fall as she ran, calling, 'Caddy! Caddy! Caddy!'

Never before had Caddy been hugged in front of such a large audience. She stared at them in amazement when her mother at last let her go. What was the matter with everyone? she wondered. Her mother was mopping her eyes and blowing her nose on blue hospital paper towel. Other eyes and noses were being dealt with too. The audience were all either smiling or mopping or waving folded newspapers. Everywhere tears. Everywhere smiles. Everywhere waves.

Is this what hospitals are like when there are no visitors? Caddy asked herself. What was the matter with these people? Were they all, like the porter, completely cracked?

The numbers were growing. Nurses. Men in white coats. A whole lot of ladies in dressing gowns and slippers who were passing round tissues like you might pass around chocolates, whispering, 'Oh thank you!' 'Oh, I shouldn't.' Eve was plunging in and out of waves of wet blue paper towel like a bedraggled mermaid in a paper sea. Footsteps were pounding fast up the corridor. Caddy turned to meet them just in time to be charged full tilt by Indigo and Saffron, wielding Old Panda. Behind them came her father, and last of all, the lunatic porter, escaped from his desk.

It was the lunatic porter who explained everything.

'Autograph, please, young lady,' he demanded, handing her first a hospital shop newspaper, and next a hospital shop pen.

That was when Caddy saw for the first time:

Cadmium Casson, the Bravest of the Brave
(over)
Ruby's Birthday Photograph

'I gave her that picture!' said Saffron proudly, pounding the paper with her fist. 'That newspaper lady! I fetched her the photograph and me and Indy told her what to put!'

'It was about the spider under the sink,' shouted Indigo, 'and about when you killed that frog. And we showed her the graves! Did she write it all down?'

But it seemed she had not written any of it down.

She had written about speeding lorries and Ruby falling and Caddy leaping to the rescue. She had added extra photographs too, blurry because they were taken on mobile phones. Ruby sprawled face down in the road. Caddy as she dragged her to safety again. Shocking photographs that made Saffron and Indigo stare in horror, and Eve say, 'I can't look! I can't think about it.' Photographs that seemed to make people want to reach out and pat Caddy, as if to check she was real.

Caddy didn't like that, and she shook her head when people offered her pens to sign their papers, copying the lunatic porter. He suddenly presented her with a pink-wrapped bunch of daylight robbery hospital carnations like a magician producing flowers from a hat. Scattered applause followed the carnations, and the clamouring sound of people reading aloud to their neighbours, and the word 'heroine', and her father turning to her suddenly and saying with unheroic honesty, 'Another time . . . another time, Caddy . . . Don't,' and her mother protesting, 'Bill! Oh, you can't say that!' and her father replying, 'Each man to his own.'

It made no sense to Caddy, and it aggravated Saffron, all this fuss for Caddy when she had had no attention for ages and ages. No breakfast either, just rushed out of bed and hurried to the hospital the moment the porter rang. 'I'm Ruby!' cried Saffron rolling on the floor. 'Help! Help! Indy, make Old Panda be the bloody lorry!'

'Good Lord in Heaven,' said Bill, and pulled her up very abruptly, causing her to roar.

'Breakfast time,' said Indigo and stuck out a tongue covered in chewed carnation petals.

Suddenly Caddy, to her great relief, discovered that she was no longer the focus of attention. She could stand back from the confusion and look around. She turned to scan the corridor, and the doorways, and the long glass windows of the hospital wards.

As she looked she became aware that somebody was watching her.

Somebody quiet.

Caddy turned and turned, searching, and then through the window that had been behind her she found what she was looking for.

Smoky dark unblinking eyes.

A solemn friendly gaze.

A mouth curved into the start of a smile.

It was a baby.

The baby and Caddy looked at one another. Deep, deep, deep, each into the other's thoughts. And Caddy did not need to see Eve's sketch book on the stand close by, nor the cards that Saffy and Indigo had made, nor the photographs from home, to know that this was the fledgling. The firework baby. The last and best touch of the genie's finger on Caddy's spinning world.

A name card was fixed to the side of her cot.

'Rose,' read Caddy.

Chapter 25
A Beginning

The baby was coming home today, that day, as soon as the surgeon who had performed his miracle had had one last look. The purple fledgling was gone. It had flown from its nest of wires and tubes. It took part of Caddy with it.

The part of Caddy that was afraid of the genie left, and it never came back. Somehow, while she had waited for the baby to live or die, she had learned that a genie was not the only spinner of worlds. Anyone could do it. She could do it herself. And so could doctors and lorry drivers and sheepish ones on doorsteps. Friends and enemies. Sisters and brothers. Fallen birds and firework babies.

'We meant it for a surprise, about coming home today,' Eve told Caddy. 'We were almost sure, I was hoping and hoping . . .' ('*Don't set your hopes too high,*' Caddy remembered) '. . . but just in case it couldn't happen we tried to keep it secret. Only somehow Saffron and Indigo knew.'

'They always know,' said Caddy.

'Fireworks today,' said Saffron, 'but first I've got to take Daddy shopping. Before he goes back to London.'

Nobody looked even slightly surprised, except Bill, who gave Saffron a very startled glance, began to speak, and then stopped. He understood, as well as Caddy and Eve, that Saffron and Indigo always knew, and he thought that perhaps it was not sensible to ask how. He had never really managed to stop Saffron answering his phone calls from London.

'All right, Saffy,' he agreed meekly. 'As soon as Eve and Rose are home we'll go shopping.'

That took longer than anyone had expected. It was mid-afternoon before the baby was finally discharged and home. By that time Saffron's father was so sick of hospitals that he was as eager as Saffy to be off.

'Come on, Saffron,' he said. 'Let's hit town!'

Saffron took charge. They bought sparklers first, 'Because there weren't any in your wardrobe,' Saffy explained. Then a great deal of proper food in tins and packets, and all the dozens of things that they thought a baby might need. Or that Saffron thought a baby might need. There was a particular sort of bracelet made of silver and glass beads owned by every single girl that Saffron knew, except herself and Caddy. Some girls had two or three.

'Me and Caddy and Rose could manage with just one, to share,' said Saffron. 'Or should we get Caddy a hamster? She's always wished she could have one. Did you know that Indigo has wanted a Doctor Who Sonic Screwdriver Torch *all his life*?'

Indigo spent the afternoon guarding Rose and Eve. The baby was in a sort of basket thing, beside the sofa. When Eve went to sleep Indigo took up position beside the basket.

'I'll watch she doesn't get out,' he promised Eve, but when his mother was safely asleep the baby did get out, extracted by Indigo himself. He lugged her around the house and garden, showing her the important places. She took a great interest in the square corners of his latest hole, gazing at them intently for a long time, while Indigo went pink with pleasure. She was safely back in her basket though, long before Eve woke up.

'You don't tell, and I won't either,' said Indigo, and Rose's eyes gleamed with the merriment of suppressed secrets.

'It would be best if you went to sleep,' advised Indigo, and she went instantly sleep.

It was the start of a great friendship.

Caddy did not stay long at home. She could hardly wait to see her friends and tell them the news. Up and down the familiar streets she ran, banging on doors.

Ruby, who had not wanted to be saved.

'Ruby! Ruby! Ruby! Ruby!'

Ruby, and all four of Ruby's grandparents, sprang on Caddy and dragged her inside. They weighted her down with the fat cat Wizard while they told her what they thought of her. It was all very flattering, but Caddy could not stay to hear it. She tipped Wizard on to the floor, told the grandparents, 'It was easy. It only took a moment,' seized Ruby, and dragged her away. 'Come with me to get the others. I've got something to show you!'

'Beth! Beth! Juliet!'

'*I hate you for ever,*' Beth had screamed at her.

Beth had no talent for hating people. Her for ever had lasted for about as long as it had taken Caddy to get out of earshot. Now when she saw her friend she flung her arms around her.

'Hurry!' urged Caddy. 'You too, Juliet! Rose is home! We just need Alison. Run!'

'We've something to tell you about Alison,' said

Beth, as they raced down the road. 'You weren't at school today, Caddy, so you don't know.'

'I know about her and Dingbat!'

'You don't know all of it though, just the beginning.'

'None of it matters,' said Caddy, and she called under Alison's window. 'Alison, Alison! Are you still grounded till the end of time?'

A girl with very short straw-blonde spiky hair glanced out of the window, vanished, and a moment later came sauntering into the street.

'*ALISON! It looks wonderful!*'

'I know,' said Alison. 'I had it done last night.'

'You should see Dingbat's hair though!' Ruby told Caddy. 'Dingbat dyed his pink!'

'*Pink?*'

'To be like Alison,' said Beth.

'So that he could say, "I love your hair! It's just like mine!"' said Alison, scornfully.

'But I thought, you and Dingbat . . .'

'Oh thank you,' said Alison. 'Thank you very much, Cadmium Casson! As if I'd go out with anyone who'd just dumped my three best friends!'

'Wouldn't you?'

'Would you?'

'I might,' said Caddy. 'I might have done, if it was

Dingbat. Poor Dingbat, what will happen to him? With none of us, what will he do?'

It was not often that Alison considered anyone's feelings, but she did now. There would be time enough tomorrow, she decided, to break the news to Caddy of Dingbat and the identical midget twins in Year 8. How they had sympathised with his loneliness, admired his betrayed pink curls, smirked identical smirks into his wicked green eyes, and begun illuminating his name on their jotters.

Later, thought Alison. Not now.

She changed the subject completely by saying, 'I've seen your baby, by the way!'

'You have?'

'Your brother had it outside. He dropped it once or twice . . . he couldn't seem to get a grip.'

'WHAT!' shouted Caddy, and raced home in a panic, and there was Rose, fast asleep and only slightly muddy, with Indigo still on guard. Then Bill and Saffron arrived, with all their wonderful shopping, and by the time it had been exclaimed over Rose was awake and ready to be properly admired.

'I'll show you the most amazing bit,' said Saffron and unwrapped Rose like a parcel to point. 'That's where they cut her open, to fix her broken heart!'

'Oh, fantastic!' sighed Juliet, enviously.

'*Jools!*' said Beth reproachfully.

'It was awful,' said Caddy, but Eve said, 'It's over now,' and gave Caddy a hug.

'Fireworks soon,' said Saffron, 'as soon as it's night.'

'It's night now,' said Indigo, and it nearly was, darkish anyway.

'How many fireworks?' asked Juliet.

'One,' said Indigo.

'*One!*'

'One bloody enormous one,' Saffron told her proudly. 'Me and Indigo have seen it already. We found it yesterday. We were just checking to see if Daddy had locked anything new up in his wardrobe . . .' (Her father groaned) '. . . and there it was! Come and show Juliet, Daddy!'

Bill was finding it difficult not to do as Saffron commanded that day, so he got to his feet as he was ordered, and showed Juliet the firework. It was as big as Rose, and would fire off three dozen explosions, Bill promised, of increasing beauty and astonishingness. For safety and steadiness it needed to be half buried in a good deep hole . . .

'The hole's all ready,' said Indigo with pride. 'Daddy showed us how big it had to be yesterday, and me and Saffy dug it. It was a secret . . . Caddy?'

'What?'

'Did you wake me up in the middle of the night?'

'Yes.'

'Were you having bad dreams?'

'Yes.'

'Have they gone now?'

'Yes,' said Caddy, with her arms around Rose.

Whistling comets streaming colours, gold and pink and green. Rockets like dragons in claps of purple thunder. Silver stars that turned to flowers and opened over half the sky. Fire jewels in fountains: ruby, diamond, emerald, sapphire, falling like rain.

'That's it,' said Bill, when the last spark faded, and the guests had gone home. 'Thank the good Lord in Heaven! Bedtime for everyone at last! The end!'

The end? Caddy asked herself sleepily, later. The last quiet hour of the day had come and she was curled up on the sofa, waiting for her turn in the bathroom. Saffron and Indigo were already upstairs. Saffron was in the bath, with Bill to make sure she stayed there. Eve was reading to Indigo, the words came floating down the stairs. 'Once upon a time . . .'

'Not the bears,' implored Indigo. 'Not that beanstalk one. Not how–the–camel–got–his hump, we did that at school.'

'Once there was a genie who was trapped in a bottle,' read Eve. 'And they put the bottle on to a ship and sailed to the deepest part of the sea, and when they arrived there they threw the bottle into the water. But the waves caught the bottle and carried it to a far-off land and flung it to the shore . . .'

'And a boy picked it up . . .' said Indigo happily.

'And a boy picked it up and he could hear a small voice crying, "I am the genie who can spin the world on its finger . . ."'

'And the boy . . . !' shouted Indigo triumphantly, '. . . let him out!'

'It used to be a girl who found the bottle,' objected Saffron from the bathroom.

'Sometimes it's a boy, sometimes it's a girl,' Indigo told her.

'Oh all right.'

That used to be my story, thought Caddy, and she thought, it really does feel like an end.

Outside in the street in front of Alison's house a SOLD board rattled in the wind. Ruby had visited the Academy, climbing with excitement the steps she had vowed she would never go near. Treacle the pony was going back to the riding stables.

But, 'The other side of the planet!' Alison had said. 'Thank goodness for you, Caddy!'

'Me!'

'It was you who sold our house at last! If you hadn't have chucked that junk about the silver Ford man would never have met your dad! That's what did it! He thought he was fantastic!'

'Oh, Alison!' said Caddy, but she had to admit, she had never seen Alison so happy. Already the ropes of boredom that had bound her for so long had tumbled away.

'You can still have friends on the other side of the planet!' said Alison.

'Of course you can,' said Caddy.

Soon Ruby would be leaving too. She had come back from the Academy with a new prospectus, a file of practice exam papers and shining eyes. Already she owned a new library card.

'It was awful without one,' she told Caddy so solemnly that Caddy had to smile.

Beth was to help out at the stables every weekend. 'And they say I can visit Treacle every day if I like. And at the weekends I get paid!'

'Paid!' said Juliet, jealously, but all the same she refrained from adding, 'Good, and don't forget you owe me a Mars bar!' After all, she was Puss in Boots with the boots to prove it, and besides she had a new interest.

'Saffron Casson is bloody amazing,' said Juliet.

It didn't feel like the end to Juliet. Nor to Alison or Ruby or Beth. Nor to Eve, unpacking her bags, or Bill looking up train times. Nor to Saffy and Indigo, now in bed and planning their Christmas lists. ('What do we need, besides fireworks and spades?' 'I think a hamster to keep the hamster company.' 'YES!')

Downstairs, the hamster, who had slept solidly since the moment of his arrival, got up to begin his night's carousing.

The baby gazed at Caddy and smiled her first smile.

Not an end, a beginning, thought Caddy.

Six Years Later
Caddy and Rose

'Look Caddy! Look what Saffron gave me! It's you!'

Caddy looked. An old photograph. Words on the back, that she read aloud.

'*Alison, Ruby and Beth and me.*'

Four girls at the seaside, arms around shoulders, sun in their eyes and wind in their hair.

'*Summer 1996*'

written underneath, in round twelve-year-old's handwriting.

Rose said, 'I wish I could remember you before you were grown up,' and Caddy laughed and asked, 'Am I grown up?'

'Compared to then you are.'

Caddy looked at the picture again. 'You're right,' she agreed. 'That's when it started. For all of us.'

'What started?'

'Growing up.'

Alison, Ruby and Beth and me.

Rose knew the names well. She had been hearing them all her life. They appeared on postcards and birthday cards and sometimes on the doorstep, bringing unexpected presents from the far side of the world. But 'Summer *1996*!' said Rose to Caddy. 'That was before I was born! Did you really truly know each other before I was born?'

'We knew each other much longer ago than that!'

'How much longer?'

Caddy didn't answer at first. She was watching the road from the window. Any minute now a driving instructor was going to haul her away for her first driving lesson. She was very, very nervous. She was almost running away, and so Rose to help was distracting her with questions.

'Can't you remember?' persisted Rose.

'I can remember exactly,' said Caddy. 'We were four-ish and five-ish. It was the first day at school. We'd never met before but the teacher sat us together at a little blue table, plonked down one at each corner . . . do I look all right, Rose?'

'What do you want to look like?' asked Rose, cautiously.

'Safe.'

'Like you won't run anyone over?'

Caddy moaned, and Rose hurried to change the subject.

'Yes you do. You look safe. Carry on! Plonked down one at each corner. Then what?'

'Did I tell you about the teacher? She was quite old, with silvery hair all twirled in loops and very tall . . . All my friends' driving instructors are ancient and awful. They have red shiny faces and hot twitchy hands.'

'If he's like that you'll see straight away,' said Rose practically, 'and then all you need to do is just say "Sorry" and don't go. Say you haven't any money.'

'It's free. First lesson free.'

'Well, we'll check through the window and if he's like that I'll go out and tell him you're dead.'

That made Caddy laugh.

'Tell me more about that teacher. So I can draw a picture.'

'She had black beads. Dangly ones, and there was a sort of purple haze about her . . . it might have been a cardigan . . .'

'Scary?'

'A bit. She came over and looked down at us. Alison was sulking, and Ruby was sucking her thumb. I was all a mess because I'd rushed in late. But Beth was perfect . . . It was so good, Rose, because we were the ideal combination. If we wanted someone perfect we pushed Beth forward, and if we wanted someone clever we had Ruby . . . Should I take a hamster? Yes or no?'

'No. You've forgotten Alison. What use was she?'

'Alison was wonderful because she hated everyone.'

'What about you?'

'I was just Caddy, most of the time. Let me see your picture . . . yes, that's what she was like! She stood gazing down at us, Alison, Ruby and Beth and me, and she said, "You four will be friends!" Just like that! Like a charm!'

'She sounds like a witch.'

'She might have been a witch,' agreed Caddy, staring from the window. 'Rose! There he is! There he is! There he is!'

'Awful?' asked Rose, and she put down her pencil, all ready to rush outside and explain that Caddy was dead.

'NO!'

'No?'

'Absolutely gorgeous!'

'Caddy! What are you doing?'

Caddy, at the speed of light, was undressing. Off came her safe blue jeans, and on went the tight black ones, still damp from the washing machine. Off came the sensible jacket and on went a tiny snow white cardigan with most of its buttons undone.

'Absolutely, absolutely gorgeous,' said Caddy, waving out of the window with one hand and putting on lipstick with the other. 'I'll take the hamster after all! Oh Rose! Say good luck! I may faint!'

'Good luck!' said Rose. 'Don't faint! Don't crash! Don't run anyone over! You look lovely! Not safe at all!'

'I hope he likes me!' said Caddy, hugged Rose and was gone. She left the door wide open, a sparkle of glitter powder and a trace of perfume like flowers.

'Don't worry. He'll love you!' said Rose.

If you enjoyed *Caddy's World* read on
for more stories about the Casson Family in
Saffy's Angel

Chapter One

When Saffron was eight, and had at last learned to read,
she hunted slowly through the colour chart pinned up
on the kitchen wall.

It was a painter's colour chart, from an artists'
materials shop. It showed all the colours a painter could
ever need. There were rows and rows of little squares,
each a different shade of red or blue or green or golden
yellow. Every little square had the name of the colour
underneath. To the Casson children those names were
as familiar as nursery rhymes. Other families had lullabies,
but the Cassons had fallen asleep to lists of colours.

Saffron found Indigo almost at once, a smoky dark
blue on the bottom row of the chart. Indigo was two
years younger than Saffron. His name suited him
exactly.

'If there is one thing your mother was good at,' Bill

Casson, the children's father would say, 'it was choosing names for you children!'

Eve, the children's mother, would always look pleased. She never protested that there might be more than one thing that she was good at, because she never thought there was.

Indigo was a thin, dark-haired little boy with anxious indigo-coloured eyes. He had a list in his head of things that did not matter (such as school), and another list of things that did. High on Indigo's list of things that mattered was his pack. That was how he thought of his sisters. His pack.

Saffron was the middle one of the pack.

Saffron had to climb on to a stool to see the colour chart properly. The stool had a top of woven string that was coming unwoven, and its legs rocked on the irregular tiles of the kitchen floor.

'I can't find me,' she grumbled to Indigo, wobbling on the stool. 'I can't find Saffron written anywhere.'

'What about the rest of us?' asked Indigo, not looking up. 'What about the baby?'

Indigo was crouched on the hearth rug sorting through the coal bucket. Pieces of coal lay all around. Sometimes he found lumps speckled with what he believed to be gold. He looked like a small black devil in the shadowy room with the firelight behind him.

'Come and help me look for Saffron!' pleaded Saffron.

'Find the baby first,' said Indigo.

Indigo did not like the baby to be left out of anything that was going on. This was because for a long time after she was born it had seemed she would be left out of everything, and for ever. She had very nearly eluded his pack. She had very nearly died. Now she was safe and easy to find, third row up at the end of the pinks. Rose. Permanent Rose.

Rose was screaming because the health visitor had arrived to look at her. She had turned up unexpectedly, from beyond the black, rainy windows and picked up Rose with her strong, cold hands, and so Rose was screaming.

'Make Rose shut up!' shouted Saffron from her stool. 'I'm trying to read!'

'Saffron reads anything now!' the children's mother told the health visitor proudly.

'Very nice!' the health visitor replied, and Saffron looked pleased for a moment, but then stopped when the health visitor added that her twins had both been fluent readers at four years old, and had gone right through their junior school library by the age of six.

Saffron glanced across to Caddy, the eldest of the Casson children, to see if this could possibly be true.

Caddy, aged thirteen, was absorbed in painting the soles of her hamster's feet, but she felt Saffron's unhappiness and gave her a quick, comforting smile. Since Rose's arrival the Casson family had heard an awful lot about the health visitor's multi-talented twins. They were in Caddy's class at school. There were a number of rude and true things that Caddy might have said about them, but being Caddy, she kept them to herself. Her smile was enough.

Caddy appeared over and over on the colour chart, all along the top row. Cadmium lemon, Cadmium deep yellow, Cadmium scarlet and Cadmium gold.

No Saffron though.

'There *isn't* a Saffron,' said Saffron after another long search. 'I've looked, and there isn't! I've read it all, and there *isn't*!'

Nobody seemed to hear at first. Caddy continued painting her hamster's feet. The baby continued screaming. Eve continued explaining to the health visitor (who frightened her very much) that she had not noticed anything at all wrong with Rose until the health visitor had pointed it out, and the health visitor continued tut-tutting.

'*I can't find Saffron!*' complained Saffron crossly.

Indigo said, 'Saffron's yellow.'

'I *know* Saffron's yellow!'

'Well then, look under the yellows,' said Indigo, and tipped the whole of the coal bucket upside down in the hearth, enveloping his end of the room in a cloud of coal dust.

This made the health visitor start coughing as well as tutting.

'I don't know how you keep your patience!' she said to Eve. Her voice showed that she thought it would be much better if Eve did not. She had dropped in to weigh Rose, as she often did, and had noticed at once that the baby had gone a very strange colour. A sort of brownish mustard. She seemed to think it was a terrible thing that Rose should have gone mustard without anybody noticing. She began undressing her.

'I've looked under *all* the yellows,' said Saffron loudly and belligerently, 'and I've looked under *all* the oranges too, and there *isn't* a Saffron!'

Rose wailed even louder because she didn't want to be undressed. Her mother said, 'Oh, darling! Darling!' Indigo began hammering at likely-looking lumps of coal with the handle end of the poker. Caddy let the hamster walk across the table and it made a delicate and beautiful pattern of rainbow-coloured footprints all over the health visitor's notes.

'*Why* isn't there a Saffron?' demanded Saffron. 'There's all the others. What about me?'

Then the health visitor said the thing that changed Saffron's life. She looked up from unpicking something out of Rose's clenched fist and said to the children's mother:

'Doesn't Saffron know?'

The words fell into a moment of silence. Rose held her breath between roars. Caddy's head jerked up and her eyes were startled. Indigo stopped hammering. Eve went scarlet and looked very confused and began an unhappy mumble. A not-yet, not-now sort of mumble.

'Know what?' asked Saffron, looking from the health visitor to her mother.

'Nothing, dear,' said the health visitor in a bright, careless voice, and Saffron, who had been frightened without knowing why, allowed herself to believe this was true.

'Nothing, nothing!' repeated the health visitor, half singing the words, and then in a completely different voice, 'Good heavens! What on earth is this?'

Rose's fist had come undone, revealing that she held a tube of paint (Yellow Ochre), obviously very much sucked.

'Paint!' said the health visitor, absolutely horrified. '*Paint*! PAINT! She's had a tube of paint! This household . . . I don't know! *She's been sucking a tube of paint!*'

'What colour?' asked Indigo immediately.

'Yellow Ochre,' Caddy told him. 'I gave it to her. I didn't think she'd suck it. Anyway, I'm only using non-toxic colours.'

'Caddy!' said her mother, laughing. 'No wonder she's gone such a funny colour!'

'I'm ringing the hospital!' said the health visitor, in a voice of controlled calm. 'Wrap her up in something warm! Don't give her anything to drink! We'll go straight to Casualty . . ."

Then for a while Saffron forgot her worries while they all tried to convince the health visitor that none of Caddy's colours were in the least poisonous, and that Rose, except for needing washing, was quite all right.

'But *why* did you give it to her?' the health visitor asked Caddy.

'To make her let go of the Chinese white,' said Caddy.

'Chinese white's sweet,' explained Saffron, and then there was another fuss. While it was going on Indigo got bored and went back to his gold hunting, bashing a lump of coal so hard that pieces flew everywhere, and the baby got a chunk to suck, and the hamster jumped in fright into the health visitor's bag, and the health visitor said, 'Thank goodness my twins! . . . If that hamster has made a mess . . . I suppose this is what they call artistic . . .'

'Yes,' said Eve eagerly. 'They are all very . . .'

'You need the patience of a saint in my job!' said the health visitor as she left.

After she had gone the children's mother hunted through the kitchen cupboards looking for something for tea. While she was doing it she cried a bit because it was so hard being an artist with four children to look after, especially in wet weather when rain blew under the kitchen door and down all the chimneys and into the bonnet of the car so that it would not start and she could not get to the supermarket. She thought wistfully of the shed at the end of the garden, her favourite place in the world.

Only Rose noticed she was crying. Rose watched her with unsurprised blue eyes, enjoying the sniffs.

The kitchen cupboard was full of non-food sorts of food. Lentils and cereal and packet sauces and jam. Eve had almost given up hope when she unearthed a large and completely unexpected tin of baked beans, the sort with sausages in, a small miracle.

'Daddy must have bought them!' she exclaimed, as happy as she had been miserable a moment before.

The beans changed everything. Saffron took over the toaster. Caddy put the hamster into its cage and cleared the table. Indigo picked up his lumps of coal. Permanent Rose sucked a crust of bread and smiled at everyone and waited patiently until someone should think of scrambling her an egg. Eve stirred the beans and sausages and was grateful to Bill Casson, the children's father. He was a real artist, not a garden shed one like herself. He was such a very real artist that he could only work in London. He rented a small studio at enormous expense, and only came home at weekends. Real artists, he often explained to Caddy and Saffron and Indigo, cannot work with three children under their feet and a baby that wakes up several times every night.

'Clever, clever Daddy, buying beans!' said Eve.

'Rose could have an egg,' suggested Caddy, reading Rose's mind.

'I wonder if Dad bought anything else,' said Indigo, and he and Saffron at once began searching the kitchen cupboards themselves, hoping for more surprises. A lump of coal turned up, with a glitter of gold on it, and a bag of squashed pink and white marshmallows which they floated on hot chocolate and shared with Rose from the end of a spoon.

It was a very happy evening and bedtime before Saffron asked again, 'Why isn't my name on the colour chart? Why isn't there a Saffron?'

'Saffron is a lovely colour,' said her mother evasively.

'But it's not on the chart.'

'Well . . .'

'The others are.'

'Yes.'

'But not me.'

'I thought of calling you Siena. Or Scarlet.'

'Why didn't you?'

There was a long, long pause.

'It wasn't me who chose your name.'

'Dad?'

'No. Not Daddy. My sister.'

'Your sister who died?'

'Yes. Go to sleep, Saffy. Rose is crying. I've got to go.'

'Siena,' whispered Saffy.

Saffy had a dream that came over and over. In the dream was a white paved place with walls. A sunny place, quiet and enclosed. There were little dark pointed trees and there was the sound of water. The blue sky was too bright to look at. In the dream something was lost. In the dream Saffy cried. In the dream was the word, Siena.

Caddy's bed was close enough to touch. Saffy could tell by the feel of the darkness that she was awake.

She said, 'Caddy, how long ago can you remember?'

'Oh,' said Caddy, 'ages. I can remember when I could only lie flat. On my back. I can remember how pleased I was when I learned to roll.'

'You can't!'

'I can. And I remember learning to crawl. It hurt my knees.'

'No one can remember that far back!'

'Well, I can. I remember it quite clearly. The burny feeling it gave my knees.'

'Do you remember a white stone garden?'

'What white stone garden?'

'Siena.'

'No,' said Caddy. 'That was you, not me.'

The next morning Indigo gave Saffron his gold-speckled lump of coal, and Cadmium added an extra colour square to the top row of the paint chart, Saffron Yellow. In London Bill Casson shut up his small (and very expensive) studio midweek, and caught the first train home.

None of these things meant anything at all to Saffron. All she could think of was the terrible news that she had forced from Eve the night before. Bit by bit, while Rose slept and Indigo argued and Caddy watched and was silent, Saffron had dragged it out.

That was how she discovered that Eve was not her

mother. Nor was a real (and nearly successful) artist in London her father. Worst of all, Caddy and Indigo and Rose were not her brother and sisters.

'You're not my family,' said Saffron.

'We are!' cried Eve. 'Of course we are! We adopted you! We wanted you! Your mother was my sister! Caddy and Indigo and Rose are your cousins!'

'That doesn't count,' said Saffron.

'I'm not doing this right,' said Eve, weeping. 'There are books on how to do it right. I have read them. You were only three. You looked just like Caddy. You called me Mummy. You were so happy. Almost as soon as you arrived, you were happy!'

'Why was it a secret?'

'It wasn't a secret!' protested Eve, trying to hug Saffron (who ducked). 'I was waiting for the right time to tell you, that's all. And the longer I left it, the harder it was. I should have done right from the start!'

'Caddy knew! And didn't tell me!'

'I forgot,' said Caddy.

'Forgot!'

'Nearly always.'

'No wonder I'm not on the colour chart,' said Saffron.

Everything seemed to change for Saffron after the day she deciphered the colour chart, and discovered that her name was not there, and found out why this was. She never felt the same again. She felt lost.

'But everything is just the same,' said Bill, trying to help. 'Nothing has changed, Saffy darling. We love you just as much as we ever did. You are just as much ours as you always were.'

'No I'm not,' said Saffy.

Eve produced photographs of Saffy's mother, but they were very confusing. Saffron's mother had been Eve's twin sister. They were so alike that even Eve had to puzzle over some of the pictures before she could say who was who.

'What about my father?' Saffron asked.

This was a difficult question. Saffron's mother had never told Eve anything about Saffron's father.

'Your mummy never talked about him,' she said at last.

'Not even to you?'

'Well,' said Eve, sighing as she remembered. 'She was in Italy and I was in England. So it was difficult. I was always going to go and visit her, and I never quite did. I wish I had.'

'Was she an artist? Like you.'

'Oh no,' said Eve. 'Linda was much cleverer than me! She taught English. In Italy. In Siena. You were born in Siena, that's why I thought it would make such a good name . . .'

Saffron was not listening. She looked at the picture of her mother again and said, 'Anyway she's dead.'

'Yes.'

'Killed in a car crash.'

'Yes, darling.'

'Where was I? Did I see her dead?'

'No,' said Eve with relief. 'You were at home. At your home in Siena. With Grandad. He was visiting.'

'*Grandad!*'

'Yes. He was there when it happened. He brought you back here to us.'

'*Grandad did?*'

'Yes, Grandad did. He wasn't always like he is now, Saffy darling.'

The Cassons' grandfather was like nothing at all. He lived in a nursing home. He sat. Sometimes in summer he sat in the garden, guided there with a nurse at each side. Sometimes he sat in a lounge and looked at a television which was not always switched on. Often Eve would collect him and bring him back home with her and he would sit there instead.

Only once, in all his years of sitting had he said a word to show that he remembered anything at all of his previous life. He had said, 'Saffron.'

Everyone had heard.

'Is Grandad still my grandad?' Saffron asked Eve,

when it seemed that the whole pattern of her family was slipping and changing, like colours in water, into something she hardly recognised.

Eve said that of course he was. Just as he had always been. Exactly the same.

'But was he my grandad right from the *beginning*?' persisted Saffron, determined to have the truth this time. 'Like he was Caddy's and Indigo's and Rose's?'

'Yes,' said Eve at once, and Caddy added,

'He is *just* as much your grandad as ours, Saffy. More.'

'More?' asked Saffron suspiciously.

'Much more,' said Caddy, 'because he remembers you. He knows your name. Everybody heard. He said "Saffron".'

'Yes he did,' agreed Saffron, and allowed herself to feel a tiny bit comforted.

Caddy was the only one of the Casson children who could recall the days when their grandfather could drive and walk and talk and do things like anybody else. She told Saffron about the evening when he had arrived at the house, bringing Saffron home.

'He had a green car. A big green car and it was full of toys. He'd brought all your toys, he told us. Every crayon. Every scrap of paper. You used to pick up stones, he said. Little bits of stone. He brought them all. In a tin.'

263

THE CASSON FAMILY...

Meet **Rose, Indigo, Saffy** and **Caddy**:
Hilary McKay's Casson family are eccentric, artistic, and very, very real.

'**Entrancing**'
GUARDIAN

HILARY McKAY
Shortlisted for the Whitbread Children's Book Award
Permanent Rose
A CASSON FAMILY STORY

Shortlisted for the Whitbread Children's Book Award

978 0 340 99906 7

'*So good it hurts*'
INDEPENDENT

HILARY McKAY
Author of the Whitbread-winning SAFFY'S ANGEL
Caddy Ever After
A CASSON FAMILY STORY

978 0 340 99685 4

HILARY McKAY
Author of the Whitbread-winning SAFFY'S ANGEL
Forever Rose
A CASSON FAMILY STORY

978 0 340 98908 1

'*A wonderfully eccentric family*'
THE SUNDAY TIMES